GUNNER

Steel Patriots MC

Book FIVE

Mary Kennedy

CHAPTER ONE

Gunner Michaels stood before the military action and disciplinary review board, waiting as the four men whispered amongst themselves. His chest was laden with ribbons and medals from previous missions and deployments, fifteen years of service to his country represented by a bunch of colored thread and metal tied together. That stellar career now held in the hands of four men whom he held little respect for; whom knew nothing of what he and the rest of his team faced during this last mission.

He was a good Marine...better than good. A member of the Special Forces branch of the Marine Corps, he was the best of the best, no bullshit. He took every mission seriously knowing he protected the lives of his teammates as well as those assigned to his care. No one should be questioned about what went down with their recent mission, no one.

Sent to rescue twelve innocent little school girls stolen from their school; the team found them tortured, raped, beaten, and left hanging on the side of the cliff. Gunner and his teammates were sent to free the girls, bring them home and kill the terrorists.

They found the girls hanging from that cliff, their tiny bloated bodies being desecrated by buzzards and vultures. They cut them down, wrapped their little bodies and sent them home to their parents. Then they went in search of the terrorists.

Gunner remembered every detail of that mission...every last detail of the faces of those innocent children staring down at him in death, begging for salvation. He vowed in those moments to never have children of his own. He wouldn't subject them to this kind of world...the kind of world that allowed innocent children to be kidnapped and tortured.

The team found the men responsible for the girls' deaths inside a small hut near a river. One guard on the outside, barely even awake, taken out by the hands of his teammate Zulu. Gunner happily set the charges on that little hut, blowing it to pieces and the bodies of the soulless pathetic animals inside.

At six-foot-two and two-hundred and ten pounds of hard-earned, well worked muscle, Gunner was a capable man and more than that, he was a capable, well-trained, highly skilled killer. One of the Marine's finest. He was more than happy spending the governments money on a bullet or block of C4 on the bad guys.

Gunner's team lead, Eric "Ghost" Stanton was a Navy Seal, but the team was made up of various members of the Special Forces community. They were a team of elite warriors, hand selected by Ghost and the government to take on missions that regular teams couldn't...or wouldn't...take on.

My Title is Marine, but it is my choice and my choice alone to be a Special Operations Marine. I will never forget the tremendous sacrifice and reputation of those who came before me.

At all ranges my fires will be accurate. With surprise, speed, and violence of action, I will hunt enemies of my country and bring chaos to their doorstep. I will keep my body strong, my mind sharp, and my kit ready at all times.

Raider and Recon men forged the path I follow. With Determination, Dependability, and Teamwork I will uphold the honor and the legacy passed down to me. I will do the right thing always, and will let my actions speak for me. As a quiet professional, I will not bring shame upon myself or those with which I serve.

Spiritus Invictus, an Unconquerable Spirit, will be my goal. I will never quit, I will never surrender, I will never fail. I will adapt to the situation. I will gain and maintain the initiative. I will always go a little farther and carry more than my share.

On any battlefield, at any point of the compass I will excel. I will set the example for all others to emulate. At the tip of the spear, I will teach and prepare others to seek out, dismantle, and destroy our common enemies. I will fight side by side with my partners and will be the first in and last out of any mission.

Conquering all obstacles of mind, body, and spirit; the honor and pride of serving in special operations will be my driving force. I will remain always faithful to my brothers and always forward in my service.

Gunner recited the MARSOC code in his head as he waited for the assholes in front of him to give him the time of day.

"Sgt. Major Michaels do you believe you acted in the best interests of your team, your country, and more importantly in the interests of those children?"

"I believe that whole heartedly sir," he said staring at the man. "Those children were gone...dead because we didn't get the proper intel to arrive in time to save them. Those men...those terrorists left us no choice but to hunt them down and remove them as a threat to future victims."

"Is it your belief then, Sgt. Major, that you had no other choice but to kill the terrorists and return the dead girls to their parents?" said Admiral Crossing.

"It's not my belief sir," said Gunner. "There was no other choice. Period. Those children did not deserve to be executed, tortured, and raped. Those children didn't desire to be kidnapped. Those children had no choice in the outcome of their young lives...those terrorists did. I helped them reach the conclusion and outcome of their lives based on their actions and I don't regret it...not for one damned second...sir."

"Sgt. Major...do you regret your actions?"

"Not in this lifetime sir. I did exactly as I was ordered. Exactly. I hope that my actions gave those parents some relief knowing their daughters' killers were no longer plaguing this earth."

"Thank you, Sgt. Major Michaels," said Crossing. "You can step outside and wait with your teammates while we finish with the others."

Gunner moved into the hallway letting out a long, frustrated breath. He looked at his teammates, an anger filling his eyes and simply nodded, taking his seat. He waited as each man told his story and then Jack "Doc" Harris was called.

Because of the shitty construction of the building, they could hear everything being said inside the room and when Jack "Doc" Harris notified the members of the panel that he possessed photos of the girls, they all stirred a bit in their seats. Taking photos of prisoners, dead bodies, anything to do with a mission was strictly forbidden unless directed to do so. Doc could be placing a noose on all their necks...or he could be saving them.

Doc stepped outside the room and stared at his teammates, nodding at them to walk with him to the end of the hallway.

"Fucking hell Doc, we didn't know you had photos," said Ghost.

"I know. I took them when we were cutting the girls down. Don't ask me why...I know it's a violation but I just had this feeling and shit for luck, it paid off."

"Well," said Razor, "I for one am fucking eternally grateful. They won't court martial us with the fear of those photos becoming public. The liberals would be screaming about human rights and the conservatives would say the killing of those men was justified. They don't want to have to argue that."

"This shit is getting fucking exhausting," said Ghost. "I'm so damned tired of having to follow rules created by men who don't do the damn job anymore...or for that matter ever did the job." They all nodded as the doors of the hearing room opened once again. The MP waved them inside.

Standing before the committee, the men all removed their hats and stood at attention.

"Gentlemen, you have presented us with a dilemma, and I won't lie...it's one I hate," said Admiral Crossing. "Your work as a unit has been indisputable, but we are getting pressures from the country's' government claiming you murdered innocent men."

Gunner nearly rolled his eyes, but closed them instead.

"I didn't say I agree. However, we are tasked with making a show of...hell, I don't even know anymore. We are asking you to retire gentlemen. If you refuse, you will be dishonorably discharged. If you take the retirement, there will be no mark on your records. It saddens me to do this...to lose some of the finest men I know and that I know we need in our service."

"I accept retirement," said Gunner through clenched jaw.

The chorus was heard down the line as each man agreed, regrettably. The Admiral nodded at them, handing them their papers that would tell administration they were taking retirement effective immediately.

"You will be expected to be packed and on the next transport home within forty-eight hours. I wish you good luck men. The world needs people like you. I hope you find a way to continue to the good fight."

Gunner followed his teammates out of the building, finding a secluded, quiet spot to finally speak amongst themselves.

"Where will you go Ghost?" asked Whiskey. Ghost looked at the men he'd called teammates for the last decade. Each man was hand selected for his team, partly because he knew of their skills, but mostly because he trusted them with his life and the lives of every member of the team.

"I have a proposition for all of you. I know some of you have family back home, but nobody has an old lady that I'm aware of," he said smirking at the men on the transport.

"Well, Tango has a mule he's fond of," said Doc with a smile.

"Fuck you Doc, at least it's a female mule," he grinned. "So, what's your point Ghost?"

"My point is...when my pops died, he left me a huge piece of land. It's nothing special, but it's got an old garage on the property where he used to repair cars, bikes, tractors, shit like that for neighbors. The house burned down years ago, but pops made the barn into a pretty livable space."

"SOOO.... you want us all to live there?" asked Gunner.

"Like...share bunk beds or some shit?" questioned Zulu.

"No...I mean, yea. Look, I ride...you all know that and I know that most of you do too. What if...what if we formed our own club...motorcycle club? We pick a name, make the garage something that we can all work and maybe open a bar or some shit."

The men all looked at one another nodding. It was a good idea, but not one of them knew anything about running a business or a bar.

"I'm in," said Tango, "but I know jack-shit about operating a bar. I can fix anything with a motor, and so can most of you, but a bar? I don't know man...I know *how* to drink...just not how to mix drinks."

"Look, it doesn't have to happen right away. MCs are pretty territorial. We need to make sure we're not stepping on anyone's toes. I'm not a fan of becoming an outlaw MC, we got our taste of outlaw in that fucking shithole we just came from and it didn't do any of us any good. I'm suggesting that between the bar and the garage, we'll have two legitimate businesses. Maybe...maybe on the side we sort of informally help people."

"Help people? Like...good Samaritans?" asked Gunner.

"Sort of...I'm thinking more like we take jobs others won't...but only the ones we want to take. We find lost kids, kidnap victims, we help the old lady being screwed over by a nasty landlord...shit like that." The men all looked at him raising their eyebrows. "Look, I know we've spent our entire careers doing just this kind of shit, but now we get to do it on our terms. The shop needs cleaning up and the barn will need to be made inhabitable...adding more electrical, plumbing...but it's huge. I've got a shit ton of money saved from all my deployments and pops left me a nice little chunk of change."

"And we'd be partners?" asked Whiskey.

"Yea we'd be fucking partners…we'd be brothers asshole," he said with a grin. "Just like we are now…we'd rely on one another and do shit our way. No red tape, no governments telling us what to do. We ride our fucking bikes when we want, we take the jobs we want, we fuck who we want, and we drink 'til we can't drink no more." The men smiled in his direction.

"I'm in," said Tango.

"Me too," said Doc.

"Why the fuck not?" said Razor.

"Fuck, you know I'm in asshole," said Gunner.

"I guess we need a name," said Whiskey. "How about Steel Soldiers?"

"No fucking way asshole…I'm a SEAL, not a fucking soldier," said Tango. They others laughed and nodded. They were all from different branches of the military and loved teasing each other about the superiority of their own branch, but deep down held mad respect for one another.

"Steel Patriots," said Ghost. "The steel between our legs…and the fucking patriot spirit we all still carry."

"Steel Patriots..." whispered Whiskey. The others nodded and smiled.

"Steel Patriots it is."

CHAPTER TWO

Darby Greer was racing against the clock. She needed to get her things packed up before her ex-mother-in-law came home from her monthly garden club meeting...or was it wine club? It didn't matter, the woman was involved in more clubs than should be legal and her controlling, manipulative ways were about to end for Darby and her four-year-old daughter Calla.

Darby didn't want to live in her house, she just hadn't had much of an option when her ex-husband died suddenly in a car accident basically leaving Darby with not enough money to even feed herself and her daughter.

Darby wasn't terribly upset by his death, hell she'd barely seen him since the divorce just six weeks after the birth of their daughter. Despite allegedly sharing custody of their four-year old daughter, Clint rarely showed up at his allotted times. Clint had seen his daughter a total of eleven times since her birth. His mother had been present on every one of those visits, Darby suspecting she orchestrated each of them.

She'd accepted long ago that Clint had no interest in being a father or husband. It was stupid really...their whole relationship. Darby had been a fool falling for the muscular, model-like good looks. He asked her to dance one night while she was out with her girlfriends. They spent the entire night in one another's arms. The sex was good...better than most, remembered Darby. Six months later they were talking marriage and when she announced she was pregnant, they were standing in his mothers' living room with a minister by the weekend.

Of course, Olivia Runyon made it seem like a secret wedding planned for months, not wanting the gossips to know her new daughter-in-law was pregnant. The vile woman even told her friends the baby was born early. Hard to explain an early birth when the baby was almost seven pounds.

When Clint died, all source of income was gone for her and Darby couldn't afford the rent on her two-bedroom cottage any longer. Olivia generously offered her a place to stay so she could be closer to Calla, but it didn't take long for Darby to realize it came with a heavy price.

She wasn't allowed to date, wasn't allowed to go out with girlfriends, wasn't allowed to go anywhere without one of Olivia's trusty chauffeurs tagging along, and worse her daughter was forced to attend a pretentious daycare where children had to wear uniforms. Without even realizing it, Darby had given control of her life to Olivia.

For almost a year Darby suffered the posturing and snobbery, the belittling remarks about her weight, her hair, her clothing. She came home one day to find her entire wardrobe discarded, replaced by clothing her mother-in-law selected. Able to salvage her clothes from the trash, she promptly returned everything Olivia purchased, earning her nasty stares for a week.

Darby thought she would be stuck forever working her hourly wage job at the small bookstore downtown, living under the thumb of her nemesis. She loved the bookstore; it just didn't provide enough income for her and Calla to live on.

Then three months ago the owner of the store decided to sell and shared in the profits of the sale with her two loyal employees. It wasn't millions, but it was enough to give Darby and her daughter a new start on life.

Now all she could think of, all she wanted to do, was take what belonged to her and her daughter and start a new life away from Memphis. Finally shoving the last of her things into the suitcases, she lugged them downstairs to her car, closing the trunk. The chauffeurs were all busy with whatever club Olivia was attending today, so it was her only chance.

Pulling into the daycare she checked her daughter out early, telling the administrator she had a doctor's appointment. Darby knew the woman was a friend of Olivia's, but she hoped she would be hundreds of miles away by the time she discovered them gone.

"Where are we going mommy?" asked the sweet-faced child in the back seat. Her long brown curls were held by a big blue ribbon at the back of her head, her huge brown eyes staring at her.

"We're going on a trip honey. You and mommy are going to find a beautiful new house with just us. How does that sound?" she asked excitedly.

"Just you and me? No more Grandma Olivia?" she said cautiously.

"That's right honey, just you and mommy. Is that okay? Maybe later we can call Grandma Olivia," she said thoughtfully. The little girl sucked in her bottom lip and looked out the window. Then shaking her head, spoke to her mother.

"No...I don't need to call Grandma Olivia," she said quietly. "Just you and me mommy...like it was before."

"Like it was before sweet girl."

CHAPTER THREE

Darby stacked the last of the books on the shelf and smiled, staring at the colorful book jackets lining the long rows of shelves. Her own bookstore...*The Page Turner*. She had no idea where she was going when she left Memphis, originally thinking she might settle in Florida. When she entered the little mountain town, she couldn't believe it!

Driving through the small town, she found the building by accident, the tiny space nestled between an Italian restaurant and a coffee shop. It was pure luck that the upstairs had been converted into an apartment that was the perfect size for the tiny family of two. It took a huge chunk of her money for the down-payment and then to get the loans to purchase her inventory, but she did it. She was in business under her name...not Olivia Runyon, not Clint Runyon, not even Darby Runyon. It was hers...Darby Greer. She had her bookstore ready for opening and enough money in her savings to keep them going for about six months.

Just down the street was a small daycare center...a normal, healthy daycare center where children wore their own clothes, had time for outdoor play, and imagination. Every morning she walked her daughter to school and went back to get the store set up. She'd painted it herself, repaired the shelves, stocked the books…every detail was by her hand.

She leaned against the counter, smiling, staring at her accomplishment. Reaching behind her, she took a bite of the sandwich she'd made for herself almost two hours earlier. It wasn't easy escaping Olivia Runyon and her clutches, but she'd done it…she'd finally carved a life for her and her daughter. One in which Olivia would have no say in how her granddaughter was raised.

Darby felt a mild shaking of the floor and then a rumble, like the sound of engines close by. Standing at the big display window, she noticed six motorcycles stopped at the traffic light. The thundering sound of the engines made her insides shake just a bit. The men all seemed big, bigger than the average man, the sleek machines between their legs gleaming in the midday sun. Their leather vests had a patch on it, but she couldn't read it from where she was standing.

She knew from her neighbor in the restaurant that the club wasn't a bike club mixed up in illegal things. They were the good guys according to the townspeople. They helped others, had legitimate businesses, and just all round did good for the community.

Darby continued to stare when one of the riders turned, looking in her direction. She knew he couldn't see her through the window, but it was as if his eyes penetrated the dark glass, glaring in her direction. She felt a shiver run up her spine as she took in the five-o-clock shadow, the full lips, the rippling of muscles in his forearms and the way his jeans hugged his hips and thighs.

"Down girl…been there…done that," she whispered to herself. It had been nearly four years since she'd had sex with anyone other than herself and even that was mild and contained considering she had a child in the other room, or a snooping mother-in-law. Something about that man made her insides melt. When he pulled away at the light, she let out a long slow breath, returning to the work she still needed to complete.

Her grand opening was just a few days away and she wanted everything to be perfect. Three hours later Darby left the store to pick up Calla, treating her daughter to an ice cream cone on the way back. When they entered the store, Darby knew immediately that something wasn't right. She ordered Calla upstairs and to lock the door.

Darby looked between the shelves, not noticing anything out of order. Finally heading back to the front counter, she spotted the envelope on the floor. She heard a shuffling behind her and then a hard push. She stumbled to her knees, her hair falling in her eyes as she caught the sight of work boots running from the building.

Darby stood, her heart racing and ran upstairs to be sure Calla was okay. When she found the little girl coloring at the table, her big smile telling her all was okay, she went back downstairs, picking up the envelope, she carefully opened it and read:

Give me what's mine...you can't hide

"Damn," she muttered. Time for some self-defense classes.

CHAPTER FOUR

Gunner watched as Ghost strapped JT to his chest in the baby carrier. Jack Tyran, or JT, was the three-month-old son of his team lead Ghost, and his wife Grace. A totally unexpected surprise for both, it would most likely be their one and only. JT kept his parents moving and Ghost more than once fell asleep at the dinner table with his teammates. Grace, the far more experienced parent took everything in stride, relishing in this gift of being a parent again.

Gunner laughed as the big, burly biker and ex-SEAL walked out with the baby and his wife. Turning, he noticed Zulu staring at his phone screen. Quietly sidling up behind him, he looked at the screen to see Zulu's very pregnant wife, Gabi or Angel eyes as they called her.

Gabi was huge...literally looking like she could give birth at any moment. She was only at thirty-two weeks, but was already on bed rest, with Zulu waiting on her hand and foot. Because he had to be at the gym, he installed cameras so he could watch her all day, calling her to fuss if she got out of bed.

"Why the hell don't you just go back to the house and sit with her and stop spying on the poor woman?" asked Gunner.

"Fuck you, asshole," growled Zulu. "You find the love of your life and then realize you've impregnated her with not one, but two very large babies and see how calm you are. Besides...she doesn't want me there; she says I make her nervous." Gunner laughed, shaking his head.

Gunner tried to limit his exposure to the eternal marital bliss cloud that hung over the club. He had a full slate of clients at the gym and no time for all the couples bullshit being thrust in his direction.

Many of his clients were women who wanted a chance to flaunt their bodies in front of the single muscle-bound marine. He never mixed business and pleasure, always politely turning them down. Most were married, which made him feel sorry for their husbands. Some were just lonely widows or divorcees. His favorite clients were two seventy-year-old sisters who made him laugh and brought him cookies.

This morning he was interviewing a new client who wanted to not only be in better shape, but also wanted to learn to fight. He would handle the physical fitness and let Zulu train her for the fighting, although he was capable of doing it all.

It was a strange call when she contacted him yesterday. She seemed nervous and unsure of what she even wanted, sounding seriously distracted. It took every ounce of patience he had to get her to answer

his questions and finally tell him that she simply wanted to become more

physically fit and learn to fight.

He suspected those weren't her only reasons, but he would give

that to her for now. He looked at the clock and noted that she was

already a few minutes late, not something he tolerated. Walking back

toward his office he checked his phone to be sure she hadn't called and

cancelled.

As he walked back to the front desk, his heart stopped in his

chest. Nothing...nothing could prepare him for the woman standing in

front of him. Wearing a body-hugging floral summer dress and strappy

high-heeled sandals, she had short black hair cut in a severe bob, falling to

the tops of her shoulders. Her eyes were an exotic, almond shape; the

rich brown framed by thick, full black lashes. Her mouth was full and

pouty, the red lips so luscious he shifted to move his hardening dick to the

side.

Her skin was the color of honey, like liquid gold. Judging by his

six-foot-two, she was probably five-feet-five but she was all lush fucking

curves, from her full breasts, to her tapered waist, down to the scrumptious hips and thick thighs. Holy fucking hell...he'd just sighted a goddess.

"Hello?" she said waving a hand in front of his face. "Did you get yourself a good look? It's not polite to stare you know."

"Sorry beautiful, but we don't get a lot of gorgeous women in here," he said giving her his best sexy smile. She looked around the room and gave him a perturbed look, waving her arm in a big circle.

"You have an entire gym full of beautiful women...all staring at you slick," she said sarcastically. "I'm here to meet with Gunner Michaels. Can you let him know that Darby Greer is here?"

Lucky fucking stars are in my sky. Son-of-a-bitch, this is my new client? I need to keep my dick in my pants long enough to get to know this woman.

"You're in luck. I'm Gunner Michaels," he said smiling down at her, his big arms flexing as he reached out his hand to shake hers. She looked at him, her gaze perusing up and down his deliciously muscular body, her mouth opening and closing.

"Nope...no thank you," she said turning and walking out the door.

"What the hell was that?"

CHAPTER FIVE

"Fuck if I know," said Zulu watching the woman race out the door. "Well don't just stand there, go get her!"

Gunner pushed the door open, seeing the woman head to a well-used Jeep, the top off, it's wheels dirty and desperately needing a wash.

"Hey! Hey wait!" said Gunner running toward her. "I'm sorry...if I said anything...did anything to offend you, I'm sorry."

Darby stopped, turning to face the Adonis she'd just run from. Damn him for being so good looking. How in the hell was she to remain professional and focused if he was going to be her personal trainer? She couldn't...she just couldn't.

"It's not you. You didn't say anything wrong...it's me," she said staring up at him, her face flushed from embarrassment and the exertion of racing out of the gym.

"Isn't it a little early for the 'it's not you it's me' speech?" he said smiling.

"See that...that is why I can't stay," she said pointing to his face. Gunner just shook his head. What in the hell was wrong with this woman? She was hot as fuck, but damn...what a fruitcake.

"I'm really not following here. Look, you called asking about self-defense classes. There must be a reason for that. We're the best in the area or you wouldn't be here. Why don't you come in and tell me what's going on and we'll go from there?"

Darby looked at the man once again and shook her head. She shouldn't be judging him on his appearance because of Clint. He seemed nice and certainly didn't give off the rich boy vibe that Clint did.

"Okay...just...just talk," she said. Gunner nodded, wondering what the hell happened to this woman to make her so skittish of him.

"Have you had a bad experience with a biker before?" he asked.

"A biker? Oh...the club...no, no nothing like that," she said following him into his office. "Listen, I'm really sorry...this is embarrassing. My ex-husband was into fitness...thought of himself as Gods' gift to women and the gym, and it definitely played in his favor. He was all external substance but nothing internal. I'm sorry I judged your physical appearance based on him. That's my issue, not yours."

Gunner nodded watching the woman twist her hands in her lap. She was nervous as shit and he hated that, but more than anything he wanted her to like his body, not hate it. He worked hard to maintain his muscle mass and physical fitness, not because he was vain, but because it was important to him and the safety of his team.

Hell, if he were honest, he wanted her to want to climb his body, but he also didn't want to live into the stereotypical asshole her ex had been.

"It's okay Ms. Greer. Let's start over. I'm Gunner Michaels one of the owners of the gym and the lead personal trainer. I'm a retired Special Forces Marine, which is partly why I maintain my fitness and take it so seriously. I'm also a member of the Steel Patriots." She gifted him with a smile so white he nearly came in his sweats.

"Hello Mr. Michaels, please just call me Darby...and thank you for taking my call about this. I...I'm new to the area and live alone with my daughter." He raised an eyebrow. Shit! She had a kid.

"Is that why you want to learn self-defense?" he asked.

"No...yes...I don't know. I'm opening a bookstore on Main Street," she said swallowing.

"The Page Turner? I saw it when I was out riding the other day," he said grinning at her. Damn! He was the sexy ass biker she practically drooled over through her window.

"Yea, that's me. Anyway, I picked up Calla…that's my daughter…from daycare the other day and came back to the shop. I felt…I don't know like something was wrong. I sent her upstairs to lock the door behind her, we live in the apartment above the store. When I turned, I saw an envelope on the floor, I bent to pick it up and someone shoved me hard."

Gunner was not liking this story one fucking bit. His protective instincts were suddenly on overdrive and he was already formulating a plan to protect Darby and her daughter.

"I wasn't really hurt; I mean bruised knees but that's all. The note said *Give me what's mine…you can't hide*."

"Do you know what that means?" he asked. She bit into that plump lower lip and his stomach did a few backflips.

"I…I think it could be my ex-mother-in-law. Her son…my ex…was killed in a car accident and I was forced to move in with her for a while, I just couldn't make ends meet. She's…well she's very controlling. She's wealthy and well known in social circles in Memphis. Olivia wanted to control everything in our lives and it was suffocating. I packed up and left about a month ago and ended up here," she looked at the man across from her swallowed. "I can't believe I just told you all of that. I'm so embarrassed."

Gunner couldn't stand the shame covering her face. He stood and moved to the other side of the desk, taking the seat beside her.

"I'd like to put my arm around you if that's okay Darby...just offering some comfort," he said. She nodded leaning into him and it was as if the world told her, it was okay now. She started crying and nothing Gunner did could stop it. Her sobs were cracking every wall he'd placed around his heart. Finally lifting her from the seat, he settled her on his lap.

The door opened and Zulu came in with a raised eyebrow. He stepped out for a few minutes, returning with water and tissues. He plopped himself on the corner of the desk and waited.

"Darby? Darby honey can you look at me?" asked Gunner.

"Oh my God...," she sniffed, "I'm s-so sorry...so embarrassed." She hiccupped.

"Don't be embarrassed beautiful," said Zulu. "Seems to me you had something to get off your chest. I'm Zulu…Quincy Slater, but they call me Zulu. I'm the other owner of the gym and I handle the boxing/fight side of the gym." Darby nodded as she took a drink of water and then realized she was sitting in the lap of Gunner Michaels.

She tried to stand, but he held her firm.

"Just relax Darby," said Gunner. "Collect yourself and then you can get up. Let me fill Zulu in on why you're here, yeah?" Darby nodded, enjoying the feeling of her bottom nestled against the hard thighs of Gunner. He casually explained everything that happened to Darby and when he got to the part about the intruder in the bookstore, Zulu's eyes blazed with anger.

"Maybe we put a man on the store," said Zulu.

"Wh-what? No…no I can't afford that," said Darby standing quickly. "Listen, I appreciate you letting me have my nervous breakdown in front of you instead of my daughter, but I can't afford security and I can't let this stop me from living. Every penny I have is invested in that store. I have to make this work."

"Understand beautiful," said Gunner, "but we won't charge you a thing. We just want to keep you safe and we can help by teaching you some basic self-defense and providing another set of eyes on the store."

"I can't let you do that. Please...just help me with the self-defense," she pleaded.

"That's a given," said Zulu. "But I wish you'd reconsider our offer for extra security on the store. At the very least let us set up some cameras on the exterior."

"H-how much would that cost?" she asked.

"Why don't you let me come down to the store and take a look?" said Gunner. "I can let you know the most likely points of entry and we'll give you an estimate from there."

"Wait you run a gym, you're part of a motorcycle club and you do security?" she asked. Gunner shrugged his shoulders staring down at her, the beautiful brown eyes of hers still filled with unshed tears.

"What can I say gorgeous, I'm multi-talented."

"Don't call me that," she whispered, "please just call me Darby."

Gunner nodded but didn't agree to shit. She was gorgeous or beautiful or anything he wanted to call her. She might not know it yet, but she would be his.

"When is a good time for me to see the store?" he asked.

"Oh...umm...any time is fine. I'm there from ten to four every day. On the weekends I have a couple of college girls working the store."

"Okay, I'll be there tomorrow at ten. In the meantime, let's walk you through what we can do for you at the gym."

"Sure, but can I use the restroom first?" she asked. Zulu pointed her to the ladies dressing room and encouraged her to check out the showers and spa facilities.

"You believe it's random?" asked Zulu to Gunner.

"Not for a fucking minute. I think the old lady is probably trying to scare her, but putting hands on that beautiful woman? That'll get you a bullet between your eyes from me." Zulu smiled at his friend nodding.

"Charming as always Gunner...it's why I love you brother."

CHAPTER SIX

Gunner woke with an enthusiasm and energy he hadn't anticipated. A certain dark-haired beauty filled his thoughts and all he could do was smile like some love-sick schoolboy.

He showered, thinking of the raven-haired beauty who walked into the gym yesterday. Normally he would fall for the long-legged blondes with silicone filled chests and air-filled heads who were always good for a quick tangle in the sheets and a note goodbye, but this one caught his attention right away in very different ways.

The summer dress she wore was unintentionally revealing and sexy as shit without effort. Her big brown eyes were exotic, those thick lashes fanning against her golden skin. The strappy sandals she wore showcased those full, gorgeous as fuck legs, her bright blue toes peeking out the tops.

Fuck...when have you ever noticed a woman's' toe polish?

By the time he left the shower his dick was ready to pound nails. He hadn't been this hard for a woman he barely knew in...well...in ever. He slid his boxer briefs on and the soft cotton caressed the sensitive skin of his dick. Knowing he would embarrass himself; he slid the boxers back down and laid on his bed, stroking his cock up and down thinking of Darby.

She looked so fucking beautiful on his lap, her curvy, plump ass parked against his groin. He desperately wanted to rub her against him. As he let her cry, he couldn't help but look down and see the deep crevice of cleavage between those full natural breasts. This was no woman made up of plastic, she was all natural and that turned him the fuck on.

Gunner felt his balls tighten and the tug in his gut as the hot cum squirted all over his stomach. His chest rose and fell with exertion as he looked down to the see sprays of thick, white creamy cum on his abdomen. He'd love to see her tongue lapping that shit up. His cock jerked and he cursed himself for thinking thoughts that would make him hard once again.

Cleaning himself, he finally dressed, and he headed to the restaurant for breakfast. Zulu and Gabi were seated, her feet firmly planted across his lap, her swollen ankles looking almost painful.

"Good morning Angel eyes," said Gunner, "how are you feeling this morning?"

"Like a beached whale...but other than that...I'm peachy," she said smiling up at him.

"Well, you look beautiful." Gabi eyed the man watching him fill his plate, grinning the entire time. As he took his seat across from her, she continued to watch his cheery disposition.

"What's going on?" she asked Zulu and Gunner. "What's happening here? You're in nice jeans, a button-down shirt, your hair is cut...oh my God! You met someone!"

"No, I didn't," he growled.

"Yes, you did!" she said sitting up.

"Baby...leave him alone okay. It's not what you think. There was a woman who came in the gym yesterday that needs help...that's all. She's all alone with a little girl and we're gonna try and help her."

"Oh wow, is there anything I can do? Is the little girl, okay?" asked Gabi. Gunner and Zulu both shrugged their shoulders.

"Don't know. As far as I know the kid is okay, but someone is trying to scare the mom. She's opening a bookstore downtown and someone got physical with her the other day."

"That's awful! Well, I'm glad she has the Steel Patriots in her corner. Let me know if she needs anything at all. Although I'm not keeping fulltime hours yet at the clinic...thanks to my constant guardian," she said looking sideways at Zulu, "I'm happy to see her or her daughter if she needs it."

"I'm not a constant guardian babe, I'm your husband and I have a right to worry about you," said Zulu.

"I know you do baby." Gabi kissed him, winking at Gunner. "Why don't you invite her to the barbecue tomorrow? I bet her and her little girl would love to get to know some of the town."

"Maybe," said Gunner standing. He didn't want to tell Gabi he already planned on asking her that very thing. He looked down at his button-down shirt and realized that maybe he was trying a bit too hard. Taking off the shirt he shoved it in his pack on his bike, wearing only the gray Harley-Davidson t-shirt and his jeans.

It was a beautiful summer morning, perfect for a ride on his bike, taking the long winding road down the mountain into town. As he pulled in front of the bookstore, he realized he was very early. Stepping inside the coffee shop next door he ordered a coffee and muffin. Turning, he noticed Darby at a table. Sitting next to her was a little girl with long dark, wavy hair, her nose down in a book, her little lips mouthing each word as she read.

He didn't want to disturb the pair, but damn they were so cute he just couldn't help himself.

"Good morning Darby," he said standing at the table. She startled and then smiled up at him.

"Oh...good morning, you're early!" she said looking at her watch.

"Curse of the military," said Gunner smiling. "I'm always early. I can sit here and wait if you like."

"No...no of course not, please join us." Gunner pulled up a chair and smiled at the woman again. "Gunner, this is my daughter Calla...Calla this is Mister Gunner, he's going to help mommy with something today."

"Hello Mister Gunner," she said staring at him with biggest brown eyes he'd ever seen. His heart literally melted.

"Hello beautiful Calla. That's a really pretty name. Are you named after calla lilies?" he asked. She smiled big, nodding her head up and down, her brown waves of hair spreading out over her shoulders.

"How did you know that? Nobody ever guesses that! The kids at school always say Callee and I have to correct them."

"Well," said Gunner leaning forward in a very serious tone, "I'll tell you a secret but you can't tell anyone." The little girl nodded, looking from side-to-side just to be sure no one was listening. Darby couldn't help but smile.

"You sure you can keep the secret?" he asked.

"I'm positive. I'm the best secret keeper ever," she said.

"Okay…my favorite flower is the calla lily." She opened her mouth shocked that the big man sitting across from her actually liked flowers. "It's true…I swear. My mom used to have calla lilies in her garden and she would cut them and put them in a vase on the table. They always smelled like fresh rain and summertime."

Gunner leaned across the table and sniffed loudly, closing his eyes.

"Yep…you're a Calla alright…like fresh rain and summertime." Calla let out a soft giggle and Gunner couldn't help himself, he smiled right along with her.

"Go wash your hands before school honey," said Darby watching her daughter scoot off toward the bathroom.

"That was very sweet of you Gunner."

"She's beautiful Darby...looks just like her mom," he said looking at the woman across from him.

"Thank you. She hasn't really had any male influences in her life. Her father didn't really come around a lot."

"That's just shitty of him," said Gunner. "I was lucky that I had a great father, an older brother and a younger one. All great male influences in my life. My mom was terrific as well, and my brothers...my teammates all have great women in their lives. I suppose I'm the rare breed that had great examples all the way around." Darby smiled, nodding her head.

"You are lucky...very lucky." Calla skipped back to the table holding her hands up so her mother could see they were clean. "I have to walk Calla to school; you can wait here or..."

"Walk with us!" yelled the little girl. Gunner looked up at her mother, his brows raised as if asking if that was okay.

"Mister Gunner may not want to walk with us Calla."

"Are you kidding me?" said Gunner. "To be seen with the two prettiest girls in the whole state? Man, I'd be a fool to not want to do that." Calla let a big smile fill her face and Gunner smiled down at her.

As they walked the sidewalk down Main Street, Darby held tightly to her daughters' hand and then noticed the little girl slip her hand inside Gunner's big, calloused one.

"I'm sorry," she whispered over her head nodding toward their joined hands.

"Don't be...seriously Darby...this is the best thing ever." Darby smiled at him again, her heart fluttering in the way she wished it wouldn't. He was just being nice, but Calla didn't know the difference and she couldn't afford for her to get hurt. Stopping at the gates of the school, Darby turned to him.

"I'll just be a minute," she smiled.

"Bye Mister Gunner," said Calla. She started to walk off and then turned, running back to him. Gunner kneeled so she wouldn't have to look up at him. "Mister Gunner will you come to the Fourth of July play? I'm Betsy Ross and it's kinda a big deal."

"Well, I can see where playing Betsy would be a big deal...I mean what would I salute if it weren't for her?" he asked in a serious tone. "I tell you what. If your mom says it's okay, I promise I'll come to your play."

"Yes!" she said with a fist bump in the air. She took off running toward her mother once again and disappeared inside the house. A few minutes later, Darby stepped out noticing all the moms eyeing Gunner as they walked by him. What she noticed more was that Gunner took no notice at all. He was completely ignoring the stares and glares.

"Sorry to make you wait out here," she said.

"No problem at all Darby...she's really something," he said smiling.

"Yea...about that...don't feel like you have to attend her play. She's just so excited to have someone other than me here...I just don't want..."

"Don't want what?" asked Gunner. Darby bit her lip looking at nothing in particular across the street. "Listen Darby, I know you look at me and see your asshole ex-husband. I understand. But I'm not him. I'm a decent, honest, hard-working guy who sees this amazingly sexy, sweet, intelligent woman standing in front of him and the bonus is she's got a little girl that's the shit!"

Darby laughed at that, nodding.

"She is that," she chuckled.

"Look, I just want to get to know you...and her."

"So...the security thing was just your way of getting to know me?" she asked eyeing him.

"Oh, hell no...you're getting the security whether you like it or not."

CHAPTER SEVEN

Gunner walked on down the street headed back to the bookstore. He heard Darby running to catch up to him and inwardly grinned.

"Gunner! Wait! Gunner you can't just force security on me," she said pulling on his hand. He took the opportunity to link their fingers and pulled her along beside him.

"I can and I will. Especially after seeing that precious little bundle of yours. This isn't just about protecting that bookstore or you, although those are very good reasons, this is about protecting your daughter."

"Gunner...Gunner I know that," she said pulling on his hand. Darby looked down realizing his fingers were intertwined with her own, and he was not letting go. "Gunner you're holding my hand."

"Yep."

"Why? Why are you holding my hand Gunner?"

"Well, you see you ran up next to me and grabbed my hand to stop me. I didn't want to stop, but I didn't want to leave you behind, so I just linked our fingers together. Now, once I did that, I discovered that I liked the way this felt, so I don't think I'm going to let go...not for a while anyway."

Darby looked down at their hands and then back up at Gunner's face. It was such a beautiful face. His dark blonde hair was cut shorter than the other day, his five-o'clock shadow still there, the curve of his muscles behind that hot as shit t-shirt making her warm.

"Gunner..."

"It's not hard Darby. I like you...and I think you like me. It's just hand-holding honey," he said pushing a strand of hair behind her ear.

"Hey Gunner baby...will you be at the gym later?" asked the tall, pathetically thin blonde standing beside them, suddenly invading their space. Gunner never released her fingers, pulling her closer to his body.

"Hi Joan, nope one of the twins will take your session today. I'm helping out my girl," he said confidently.

"Your girl?" she said with a sound of disgust. "Huh? I've never known you to have a *girl* Gunner."

"First time for everything Joan, tell your husband I said hello." He continued walking; Darby right next to him. He didn't speak until they were inside the bookstore.

"See...see that's the reason..." Gunner held up his hand to stop her.

"Stop right there honey before you say something you can't take back. That woman is married. I could give a shit if it's happily or unhappily, she's married and I don't touch married, engaged, or dating women. She's a client at the gym and she comes onto anything with a pulse. As you could tell, I wasn't interested in her...at all." He took a step closer to Darby, shoving that stray hair behind her ear again, cupping her cheek. "You are who I'm interested in Darby Greer...you."

Darby started to protest, but she just couldn't. She knew it was coming, she could see him lowering his mouth to her own, those beautiful lips touching her own, tasting her. She felt the rough whiskers against her skin and when he pulled her closer, his other hand firmly on her lower back pushing her against him, she let out a hot sigh against his lips.

"Fuck baby," he said leaning his head against her forehead. "That was the hottest thing ever."

"What are we doing Gunner?" she asked with a tear in her eye. "We hardly know one another...I...I don't know..."

"Stop thinking so much Darby," he said kissing her quickly once more before stepping back. "As I said, I like you...a lot and although you don't know me, you can ask any of my brothers and they'll tell you...I don't date...ever. You walked into that gym yesterday and nearly knocked me on my ass. I want to get to know you Darby, you and Calla. Can't we just do that?"

"Why? I mean...all those beautiful women..."

"Those women aren't beautiful honey...they're fake, and plastic, and desperate. You...shit you're strong, so fucking strong...and so damned gorgeous Darby. You take my breath away honey."

"Wow," she said feeling herself flush. "You really know what to say to a girl don't you?"

"I say the truth to the woman I want to get to know. I realize there is more at stake here than you and me Darby. I promise you I will do nothing to harm you or Calla. You have my word on that."

She looked up at him once again and took a deep breath. Did she dare hope for more than this life? Did she dare to dream there was more for her and Calla? Taking a step forward she stood toe to toe with

Gunner, her five-feet-five in her sandals staring up at his six-foot-two. Rising on her toes, she smiled, kissing him on his lips sweetly.

"Yes," she whispered. "Yes...I'll try."

"Thank fuck," he groaned pulling her into a hug. The front door opened, a bell above ringing and Darby blushed, pulling away from Gunner. A dark, handsome man stood in the doorway grinning.

"Hey Gunner...watcha doin'?" smiled the man.

"Tango," he growled. "Darby, this is my teammate and pain in my ass, Tango. Tango, Darby Greer."

"Hello beautiful," he smiled. "Well, that answers that question."

"What question is that?" she asked looking confused.

"Why Gunner got up and out so early this morning...he had something to get to."

CHAPTER EIGHT

Darby busied herself around the store, while Gunner and Tango perused the outside. She had a steady stream of customers for a Friday, almost everyone who entered making a purchase. Around one, she noticed that the guys were still outside and neither had stopped to eat. Darby turned the sign on the door around and walked out to speak with them.

"Hey guys, you've been busy out here. How about I pick up some sandwiches from the coffee shop?" said Darby.

"No way baby," said Gunner. "Let's all stop and grab some lunch. Can you close the shop for an hour?"

"Sure, I turned the sign, but really guys let me treat," she pleaded.

"No can do beautiful," said Tango. "You're our client. We pay for everything, it's just the way it has to be." Tango opened the door to the coffee shop and smiled at the young woman behind the counter. He'd been coming in at least three times a week just to see that fresh-faced beauty.

"Hi Tango," she said blushing. "What can I get y'all?"

"Roast beef sandwich for me with some of that homemade coleslaw. Gunner?"

"Turkey with Swiss on rye for me and I'll just have a bag of chips with that. What about you baby?" he said turning to Darby. She felt herself blush, still not used to his terms of endearment.

"I'll have the chicken salad sandwich and the potato salad."

"Great choice," said the girl behind the counter. "I'm Taylor by the way. I've been meaning to come next door and welcome you to the neighborhood."

"Oh! Do you own this shop?" she asked.

"I do. My grandparents ran it until they retired about six months ago. My dad didn't want it, but it was always my dream...so here I am."

"Well, it's great to meet you Taylor...I'm Darby. I'm sure we'll see more of each other." Taylor nodded smiling at Tango. Sitting with Tango and Gunner, Darby couldn't help but quiz the man.

"So, Tango...how long have you known Gunner?" He smiled at the woman and then looked at the pained expression of his teammate.

"We've worked together now for over twenty years. We were on the same Special Forces team, although I'm a SEAL and he's a Marine."

"Is Tango your real name?" she asked innocently.

"No beautiful," he chuckled. "My real name is Tyler Green although no one calls me that anymore. Tango was my call sign in the military."

"I'm confused…doesn't tango mean enemy or target?" she asked. Both men raised their eyebrows at Darby and smiled.

"Beautiful and smart," he grinned. "Yep…that's right. They called me that initially on a mission to confuse the bad guys…as it turned out…I'm a bit of a bad guy when in operation mode myself, so the name stuck."

"I see," she nodded. "And you and Taylor?"

"Oh…yea…no there's nothing there…she's just a kid," he said brushing it off way too quickly.

"Uh huh," nodded Darby. "Forgive me Tango, but that's no kid. Taylor is a grown woman with her own business. She's also incredibly beautiful and looks at you like…"

"...like you look at Gunner," said Tango grinning. Darby started to speak when Taylor set down the plates of food interrupting the moment.

"Enjoy your lunch," she said in a cheery voice. "Before you leave Tango, I have some of those cookies you like. I'll put a few in a bag for you to take with you." She turned and left as Darby grinned with satisfaction at Tango.

"So...what have you guys been doing on the outside of my building," she asked.

"Putting up security cameras," said Gunner taking a bite of his sandwich.

"What? Gunner! You said you would tell me how much it cost and then we would talk. I can't afford all of that...you promised me Gunner."

"I promised we would help and we are," he said shrugging. "The cameras are something we have around all the time. They link easily to an app on your phone or computer and to our systems back at Club Steel. It's not a big deal honey...I promise."

"You have to let me pay you," she said. Gunner shook his head. "Dinner."

"What?" he said looking up at her.

"Dinner tonight…I…I'll cook you dinner. That's a start in paying you back."

"You don't have to cook me dinner," said Gunner. Tango looked at the two going back and forth and could only grin at their banter.

"I…I want to cook you dinner…a-and Tango too if you want to join us," she said.

"No can-do sweetheart," he said knowing his friend would thank him later. "Got plans this evening."

"See…he can't," said Gunner. "But I accept. Tomorrow you and Calla can join us at Club Steel for a barbecue. We try to do one once a month and it brings residents from all over this part of the county. You and Calla can get to know everyone." She nodded and smiled at him.

The conversation continued until lunch was done and then Gunner and Tango went back to installing the cameras. An hour later he noticed children walking by and went into the bookstore.

"Darby? Did you need to pick up Calla?" he asked. She looked up at the clock.

"Damn! I got slammed after lunch and my help isn't here yet."

"Call the school and let them know I'm going to get Calla. Tell them to check my license and to make Calla tell them why I like her name." She opened her mouth to protest as three people lined up for check out.

"Just do it babe." Gunner went back outside to find Tango. "Hey…take a break with me and meet the coolest little kid on the planet."

Tango looked at his friend worried that he might be losing his marbles, but nodded. Following him down Main Street, they stopped in front of a daycare center. Gunner opened the gate and stepped inside.

"I'll be right back." Walking into the front reception area, he looked at the older woman and smiled. "Hi, I'm Gunner Michaels and I'm here to pick up Calla."

"May I see your license sir?" Gunner pulled out the license and she nodded. "And why do you like Calla's name?"

"Because my mothers' favorite flower were calla lilies." She smiled up at him again and pressed a button.

"Calla's father is here to get her." Gunner started to correct the woman, but for some reason chose not to. Calla came running down the hallway, her hair flying behind her with a hand full of papers. She leapt into his arms, as he swung her up against his chest.

"Hello beautiful!" he said opening the door. Tango stood wide-eyed staring at him as his friend carried the little girl toward him. "Calla, this is my friend Tango. Tango, this is the most beautiful little girl in the whole wide world…Calla."

"Hello Mister Tango," she said politely extending her hand.

"Oh sh…sugar," he grinned. "Yea…I see it now. Hello beautiful how are you?"

"Good! I made a picture for you Mister Gunner." She pulled on one of the sheets of paper, handing it him. It was a very sketchy drawing of Gunner saluting a flag and Betsy Ross in the back sewing a flag.

"Wow…that's amazing! I can't believe you made that for me. I am going to frame this and put it in my office."

"You are?"

"Of course! Why wouldn't I?"

"Jacob said you wouldn't like it because you're not my real daddy. He said I didn't have a daddy because nobody would want to love me…I…I told him you were my pretend daddy for now...that I knew the difference. He...he's mean." Gunner's face darkened and he hugged the little girl closer to his chest.

"Where can I find this Jacob?" asked Tango in a serious voice.

"I know brother," grinned Gunner. "Look at me Calla." Her big brown eyes were filled with tears and he set her down, kneeling in front of her.

"Calla, I know I'm not your real daddy. I'll never be your real daddy."

"Why not?" she said sniffling.

"Well, that's a little harder to explain, but know this. You are totally easy to love and Jacob is a fool for saying that. I may not be your daddy, but you can bet I'll be at your play and anything else you want me to attend. I think you're the most amazing little girl ever and I can't wait to get to know you better."

"Really?" she said smiling at him.

"Really," he grinned. She wrapped her arms around his neck and hugged him. Gunner barely held it together looking up at Tango who was biting his lip.

"Does that mean I can call you uncle Tango?" she asked.

"Sh…sugar…yea…you can call me uncle Tango, sweetie."

"Yes!" she yelled running toward the store. She opened the door yelling for her mother. "Mommy! Mommy! I get to call Mister Tango Uncle Tango and Mister Gunner said he'd by my pretend daddy and…."

"What?" gasped Darby looking up at the two men.

"Wait…wait before you jump…she asked if she could call Tango uncle Tango and he agreed. Some little sh…kid told her she didn't have a daddy because no one would love her. I just explained that she was totally loveable, but I also explained that I was not her real daddy, but would be happy to attend anything she wanted me to…with your approval." He let out breath seeing Darby relax a bit.

"Oh sweetie, was Jacob mean again?" she asked.

"Is this a pattern?" asked Tango.

"Sort of…I mean, you know kids they can be cruel. She's the new girl and she doesn't have a father…it's just fuel for the preschool fire."

"No excuse," said Tango. "The teacher should do something about it." Darby nodded, but knew that the men wouldn't understand.

The teacher was overwhelmed just trying to get thirty preschoolers to eat, let alone be nice to one another.

"Okay, time to close up shop...what a day! Calla? You go wash your hands and make your bed young lady. Mister Gunner is staying for dinner tonight."

"Yaaaaaayyyyyyyy!!!" Her little voice echoed as she climbed the steps and Tango and Gunner laughed.

"She's fucking amazing," said Tango.

"She is that," said Darby smiling. "So...am I all secure?"

"Yep...let me help you set up the app while Gunner picks everything up." Tango spent the next twenty minutes downloading her app and getting the settings adjusted. She had views of the front and back door, both directions on the main street sidewalk, as well as the back alley where her trash bin was located. They'd installed a camera at the foot of the staircase leading to her apartment and somehow, without her seeing them, they'd installed a top-notch lock with handprint technology for the apartment door.

"Are you sure you won't stay for dinner?" she asked Tango.

"Not this time, but you can be sure I'd love to spend some more time with that kid…she's amazing!"

"Thank you Tango," she said waving. Gunner smiled at his friend, nodding.

"I'm just gonna grab a clean shirt off my bike. Is there…is there somewhere I can just clean up a bit?" he asked.

"Of course." He grabbed the button down he took off earlier in the day and followed Darby as she locked the store and made her way upstairs to her apartment. It was small, but efficient. The kitchen was tiny, but the appliances were new. The hardwood floors were original and in great condition. The bedrooms were tiny, one fit a twin sized bed and dresser…perfect for Calla, the other had a queen-sized bed and dresser…big enough for the two of them.

"The bathroom is in there. There's clean towels in the linen closet," she said blushing. He nodded and kissed her forehead.

"I'll be right back beautiful."

CHAPTER NINE

Darby busied herself in the kitchen while Gunner and Calla played on the floor with her building blocks. That girl was made for engineering, thought Darby. Anything that could be stacked together was made bigger and better than the original.

She listened as Gunner spoke to Calla in such a sweet, loving way...praising her when she did things well and asking questions when something failed to help her figure out what went wrong. He spoke to her like a father, and for a moment, Darby felt the bubble of tears starting in her chest. She swallowed, willing them down and then turned.

"Dinner is ready you two," she grinned. Butterflies formed as she said the words. Something so innocuous, yet it felt like a moment a family would share and yet she'd known Gunner for less than forty-eight hours. Calla sat between Gunner and Darby, her little legs swinging back and forth on the chair.

"Do we have to eat by grandma's rules since we have company?" asked Calla quietly. Gunner looked at Darby, confused.

"No baby...we don't ever have to follow grandma's rules ever again." Darby filled Callas' plate and watched as she dived in to eat. "My ex...Olivia...she wouldn't let Calla eat if there was company, until they took their first bite. She was just three when we moved in and didn't know any better. There was a lot of scolding...or molding as she called it."

"That's fu...fudging cruel," he corrected himself. Darby smiled and reached over, touching his hand.

"Thank you for trying so hard with your words."

"I won't lie," he laughed, "it's not easy changing habits that I've had for forty years...well, all my adult life."

"Wow...you're forty?" asked Calla as if amazed that someone could be that old.

"I am...I'm an old man," he said using a creepy old voice. Calla laughed at him.

"You're not old Mister Gunner...mommy is thirty-one...is that the right age for her to be your girlfriend?" Gunner choked on his bite of salad and looked up at Darby whose face was white.

"Calla...that's not..."

"Yes, that's the perfect age for your mommy to be my girlfriend," he grinned. At least he got the kid on his side. "In fact, don't tell her but

I've been trying to get your mommy to be my girlfriend now for two whole days!"

"Wow…" she said with childlike awe and big eyes. "Mommy you should really say yes. Mister Gunner is super nice, and he hasn't yelled at me once like daddy did." Gunner stilled, staring at his plate for a few seconds and then looking up at Darby. A tear escaped the corner of her eye and she nodded.

"That's so…so sweet of Mister Gunner isn't it, baby. Remember mommy told you, real men don't yell at ladies or hit them."

"That's right huh Mister Gunner." He looked at Darby and swallowed.

"That's right baby…no man yells at a woman or hits her…ever." The rest of dinner proceeded as expected but when Calla let out a big yawn, Darby excused them to give her a bath and get her ready for bed. Thirty minutes later, Calla came running out in her princess pajamas and jumped up to the waiting arms of Gunner. She smelled of bubble bath and strawberries, her long hair wet, tied off in a braid.

"Goodnight Mister Gunner," she said kissing his cheek.

"Good night sweet girl," he smiled.

"Can Mister Gunner read me a story mommy?" she asked.

"Oh...I..."

"I'd love to, if mommy doesn't mind," he said smiling at Darby.

"Okay...that would be nice. I'll take care of the dishes while you do that." He nodded, taking Calla's hand and headed to her room. She grabbed a book off the shelf and handed it to him, then tucked herself between the sheets. He sat against the headboard; his big feet crossed at the ankles hanging off the bed.

"The Wishing Book," he said. "I don't think I know this one."

"Silly...it's for kids," she said with a big yawn. He laughed, nodding.

"Right...of course. Okay...I wish for things all the time...do you?" Calla closed her eyes, but nodded her head. "I wish for rainbows and popsicles. I wish for dinosaurs and dogs. I wish for butterflies and lollipops. I wish for princess dresses and football shoes."

He grinned down at the little girl. Such simple things, such sweet thoughts in a world that needed more of them. Calla never opened her eyes, but in a faint whisper said.

"I wish for a daddy." Gunner closed the book and just sat next to her until he heard her faint, soft breathing. Standing he placed the book back on the shelf and knelt to kiss her forehead. He closed the door, walking back into the living room and took a seat on the sofa. Darby looked at him and smiled.

"Let me guess...she wanted the Wishing Book?" He nodded, grinning. "I'm sorry Gunner. I should have told you she would want that. Wine?" she asked holding up her own glass.

"Beer if you have it." She nodded opening the bottle and handed it to him, sitting next to him on the sofa. "Will you tell me about the yelling...the hitting?" She let out a long sigh and leaned her head back on the sofa.

"Clint never wanted to be married. I mean we dated for a few months and I thought that's where it was leading, but...he just never wanted that. I was so infatuated with him. I mean, he was so handsome, so muscular...all the girls wanted him, but he chose me...or so I thought. When I got pregnant, I was happy. I didn't care if we got married, I just was excited to be a mom."

"Why did you...get married?"

"His mother. She's a true southern belle and no one was going to say her son had a baby out of wedlock. The second he told his mother; she was planning a ceremony and we were standing there saying 'I do'. As much as I thought I wanted that, the minute we were standing in front of the minister, I knew I didn't want it. I looked over at Clint and all I saw was..."

"Was what baby?" he said pulling her closer.

"Hate. Anger. Disgust. We didn't go on a honeymoon. His mother immediately set us up in a little house not far from her. He was working at the family law firm. He wasn't a lawyer...not really sure what he did to be honest, but from the moment we were married, he never touched me again."

"What? You mean..."

"Nothing. He would yell at me...tell me I was getting fat as my pregnancy went on. When I was eight months pregnant...he slapped me for the first time. I had no one to call...no family, so I called his mother. She immediately came over and spoke to him in the bedroom. An hour later he came out and apologized, said he would never touch me again."

"Did he?" asked Gunner already fuming on the inside.

"Yes. Calla was three days old and I was cramping...bad. I knew I needed to go back to the hospital, but he was angry because I was interrupting his football game with his buddies. One of his friends, Aaron felt bad for me and took me to the emergency room. Turns out I had a clot that nearly killed me. Aaron stayed with me that night, helping to take care of Calla. The next day his mother showed up angry that I hadn't called her."

"Fuck baby...I'm so sorry." Gunner kissed her temple, rubbing his big hands over her shoulders.

"I never saw Aaron again...not sure if their friendship suffered because of that, but I rarely saw Clint after that as well. His mother said he was taking on new responsibilities for the firm. I knew he was screwing around. I could smell it on him when he would come in at night. He never tried to touch me sexually again. When I finally found out he was seeing other women, I asked for a divorce."

"How did that go over?"

"Not well. He slapped me a few times, threatened to take Calla from me. When I threatened to leave, he punched me. He realized what he'd done and left. His mother made sure the divorce went through quickly, but he was given joint custody of Calla. At first, I wanted to fight it, but then I realized he didn't want her...he never showed up for his visits and when he did, it was because his mother was with him."

"Every once in a while, he would show up drunk and try to get into the house. That's when he would hit me. Calla...she was just three...but somehow, she remembers. The last time he came, she tried to lay over me to stop him from hitting me. Instead, he hit her. I think he shocked himself that he did that...he ran. I heard tires screeching out of the driveway and knew I needed to run. Four hours later the police were at my door. He'd died taking a curve too fast...with his dick out and his girlfriend's lips wrapped around him."

"Shit honey...I'm so fucking sorry."

"I didn't care...honestly, it didn't even matter. I was almost relieved. The problem was he left me nothing. His insurance policy was paid out to his mother. I couldn't afford the rent on the house...which she owned by the way...and I only had a part-time job at the time. I was forced to move in with Olivia. She controlled everything in my life...everything."

"How did you get away?"

"Waited. Waited until she was out of the house and her spies were gone. I packed everything that belonged to Calla and me, got a friend at the courthouse to put in the paperwork so Calla could take my maiden name and we left."

"I wondered about that...her name being Greer and your mother-in-law being Runyon."

"So that's it...that's the whole sorted tale. I left to get a better life for my daughter and freedom for me. I'm thirty-one years old. I have a bachelor's degree in history...which earns you no job offers...I spent every penny I had on that bookstore downstairs...and I'm praying it makes it because if it doesn't, I have nothing...nowhere to go."

"You will always have somewhere to go baby...I will be here for you." He looked down at her face, filled with confusion and fear and kissed her. "I know you don't believe me and that you're scared as fuck right now, but you should know after meeting Tango, I am what I say I am Darby. I'm crazy about you and that little girl and I want to see where this goes for us."

"Have you ever had a serious relationship Gunner? I don't mean to sound mean...but..."

"It's okay…I get it. I did…once. I was in love and came home from my first deployment ready to propose. She answered the door six months pregnant…I'd been gone a year. That pretty much ended that."

"I'm so sorry Gunner," she said hugging him.

"I'm not baby…it led me here…to you and to this. This is where I'm supposed to be."

"You're so sure…how…how can you…"

"Because I know what I want woman…and I want you." He held her face in his hands and took her mouth with power and passion, his tongue dancing with hers as she moaned against his lips. Darby pulled herself closer, straddling his thighs, her own on either side. His big rough hands felt their way up her thighs, pushing the skirt of her dress higher and higher, and he groaned.

"Fucking hell woman you're hot as shit," he growled. "I love these thighs baby and I can't wait to have them wrapped around me, but I know we have a little girl in the other room."

"We?" she said shocked.

"You know what I meant. You're so fucking beautiful Darby. I want you baby…like in every way a man could possibly want a woman."

"I-I want you too Gunner...I really do."

"Good...that's good enough for now. I'll pick the two of you up tomorrow at eleven for the barbecue. Why don't you bring an overnight bag for the two of you and you can stay with me at my house?"

"Are you sure? I mean a four-year-old in your house might be a little overwhelming," she grinned.

"I can't fucking wait," he said kissing her. He stood, setting her on her feet and she swayed from the headiness of the passion. "I'll see you in the morning beautiful. Sleep tight." She walked him to the door of the shop, waiting to lock it once more and turn on the security.

"Thank you, Gunner, for everything today and for...for believing in us."

"That's the easy part baby."

CHAPTER TEN

Gunner walked into Club Steel just after ten o'clock. The restaurant and bar were full of patrons, the music loud. The twins were in the corner with two girls, their tongues playing tonsil hockey with the women from the looks of it. Tango and Razor were at the bar sharing a laugh.

"Hey man," said Tango raising a beer to Gunner. "How was your dinner?"

"Fuck you," he said grinning at the man. "If you want the truth Tango...it was fucking amazing. I made fun of the guys when Grace, Bree, Kat, and Angel eyes walked in, but I gotta tell you...Darby is the one brother." Tango nodded his head as Razor looked on shocked.

"Are you telling me that Gunner Michaels...I'm single forever Michaels...has finally fallen?" said Razor.

"Kiss my ass...and yes," he grinned.

"Plus, she's got the cutest fucking kid ever," said Tango. "I have to say Gunner, if you decided to pass her up, I'd have to make a try for her myself. She's beautiful, smart, owns that bookstore, and that little girl is something else." Gunner nodded proudly.

"They're coming tomorrow for the barbecue. I'm hoping Darby meets some of the people in town, maybe drum up some business for the bookstore."

"I have an idea," said Razor, "why don't we ask Darby to carry the line of books we always recommend to new bike owners. She could be our source instead of always referring buyers to an online source."

"That's a good idea," said Gunner. "I'll bring it up with her tomorrow."

"What's the story with her ex and the mother-in-law?" asked Tango.

"Shitty story. The ex didn't want to be married in the first place, but didn't mind getting Darby pregnant. The mother made him marry her. She knew it was a mistake from the beginning. Fucking asshole started hitting her while she was pregnant. She nearly died because he wouldn't take her to the hospital."

"He dead now?" asked Razor.

"Yea. Drove his car off a cliff while his girlfriend was giving him head. Best thing in the world as far as I'm concerned, but the mother-in-law wants to control Darby, so she left pretty quickly. I'm gonna have Ace check on the old lady and make sure she keeps her distance."

"You think the old lady is the one bothering her?" asked Tango.

"Not sure...but I'm gonna find out. Headed to bed now. You boys be good and if you can't be good...be good at it."

Gunner walked out the back doors to see Grace and Ghost with the baby on the porch. He waved at them and walked along the path, finding his way to his house. Once inside, he realized it needed a good cleaning before he could welcome Darby and Calla to spend the night.

For the next three hours he washed sheets, scrubbed floors, cleaned his bathroom and kitchen, washed all the dishes, took out the trash and finally did every ounce of laundry. By the time he was done, he was exhausted but also excited to bring his girls home.

Fuck...my girls...

He lay awake for hours thinking of them inside his home...the bedroom at the end of the hall perfect for Calla, her toys lined up against the wall, maybe a built-in bookshelf for all her books and room for hundreds more.

His closet was more than big enough for Darby, the walk in was made for a couple. Not for the first time he wondered why he'd built it that way when he was a single man. Maybe he knew he would find the right one. He damned sure felt like Darby was it for him.

Falling asleep, his last thoughts were...I wish I had Darby and Calla.

CHAPTER ELEVEN

Calla was wide awake, bright and early, but knew not to wake her mother on a weekend morning. She might be only four years old, but she knew that her mommy worked hard and needed to sleep when she could, so Calla always waited like a big girl.

She sat at her little table and chairs drawing several pictures. When she was satisfied with her creations, she shoved them inside her Dora the Explorer backpack and then waited patiently in front of the television for her mother to wake up.

Darby could hear Calla moving around the tiny apartment and could only smile. She was so excited about visiting Gunner today and if Darby were honest, so was she. It was all she could think about last night as she lay there touching herself, finally rubbing her aching pussy until she felt the escape and flood of her need. Pushing back the covers she walked into the living room to see her daughter watching one of her cartoon shows.

"Good morning baby," said Darby.

"Good morning mommy! Can we go to Mister Gunner's house now?" she asked excitedly.

"Sweet girl, you have to be patient. It's barely eight o'clock in the morning. I would bet that Mister Gunner is still sleeping. He'll be here in a few hours."

"A few hours..." she whined.

"Yes," laughed Darby. She heard the chime of the front bell and looked at the newly installed app on her phone. Staring right back at her was the face of Gunner Michaels. "Or not."

"Good morning beautiful," came his sexy voice. "I know it's early but thought we'd go for a ride and get some breakfast." Darby smiled.

"I'll be right down to let you in." She looked at her daughter engrossed in her cartoons. "I'll be right back Calla, you stay here, okay? Don't move."

"Okay mommy." Darby practically ran down the stairs to see Gunner at the door in his cargo shorts, running shoes and t-shirt. He looked so damned handsome and it made her acutely aware that she had no makeup on, her hair wasn't done and she was in a little pair of sleep shorts and tank top.

Gunner looked up to see her walking toward him, her short little shorts exposing those fucking amazing legs, the thin tank top doing very little to hide her massive tits and those huge nipples pointing straight at him as if daring him to touch. Her straight black hair was only slightly messy, her face free of make-up, but those damned eyes were huge, fringed in the thick black lashes.

"Hi," she said opening the door slowly. "Sorry I didn't expect anyone here...I need to get dressed..." Gunner simply closed the door, engaged the lock and lifted her in his arms, wrapping her legs around his waist.

"You're fucking beautiful," he said growling in her ear. He trailed kisses down her neck, pressing his big hands against her ass, forcing her core to rub against his hard dick. "Fuck baby I want you."

"Me too..." she gasped pulling his hand she moved behind one of the shelves of books, shoving her shorts down, she pulled his down quickly. "Fast...now..." she said breathlessly.

"Yea...fast..." he smiled. "Condom?"

"No...yes...it doesn't matter...I'm on the pill...I haven't been with anyone since Calla was born."

"I'm clean baby...never do it without a condom...need to feel you..." She nodded as he lifted her, wrapping her legs around him once more as the head of his cock touched her wet opening, they both gave a silent moan and his cock slammed into her. "Fuuuckkkk....you're so fucking tight." She nodded, kissing him like it was the last she'd ever receive.

"Move Gunner...now...need you...need all of that big...thick...beautiful...cock..." Fucking hell this woman was going to be the death of him.

Gunner was happy to oblige driving inside her hard and furious. Her unrestrained breasts bounced against his t-shirt, her nipples huge and begging to be sucked. He wanted all of her, but knew this had to be fast, leaving no time to explore the body he'd dreamt about this time.

"Gunner...now...now..." she cried softly. He nodded, slamming into her again and again until his cock was drained and she shook and moaned with relief. Darby felt herself blush and then laughed softly. "Ummm...good morning."

"Good morning gorgeous," he said kissing her as he unwound her legs from around his waist. Darby bent to pick up her shorts and he couldn't help but give her ass a little slap. She smiled at him as he pulled his own shorts up. "You were fucking perfect Darby."

"So were you Gunner," she said kissing him again. "Come on. There's a little girl upstairs ready for you to take her to a picnic."

Gunner followed Darby up the stairs, her ass swaying in front him, he couldn't help but place his hands on her cheeks, sliding them up under the hem of her shorts, his fingers feeling the slickness of her wet hole, filled with his desire. She stopped on the steps half way up, breathing heavily as his fingers moved in and out.

Darby looked over her shoulder wanting to tell him to stop. He held a finger to his lips and she nodded. The sounds of her wetness, his juices oozing from her body were beyond erotic. His fingers were like magic, finding the spot that no man had ever found for Darby. She turned quickly, seated on the stairs and spread her legs wide as he took her mouth, continuing to scissor his fingers inside her, his thumb rubbing her magic button.

It was only seconds and Darby literally shattered against his hand; her own fist jammed against her mouth trying not to scream out in passion. Gunner removed his fingers, sliding them in between his lips, licking each one as if he'd dipped them in chocolate sauce.

"Jesus Gunner you're so damned sexy," she gasped.

"I'm nothing compared to you beautiful," he said leaning over her kissing her. She tasted them and moaned against his lips once more. "Come on...my girl is waiting." He winked at her and she nodded.

"Mister Gunner!" yelled Calla running toward him.

"There's my girl!" he said twirling her around.

"Mommy it's Mister Gunner...he came early..."

"Yes...yes, he did come early," said Darby blushing as he winked at her.

"Mommy your face is all red are you okay?" asked Calla.

"Yes, sweet girl, Mommy is perfect in fact," she said kissing her daughter's head. "I'm going to shower and get dressed. Why don't you pick out what you want to wear to the picnic and then we'll have some breakfast?"

"Need any help in there?" asked Gunner grinning. She shook her head smiling at him, but as Calla ran into her room, Darby let her fingers glide into her mouth and seductively licked them, sucking them, finally releasing them with a big pop. She looked down to see Gunner's tented shorts and smiled.

"I don't know Gunner...need any help?" she smiled.

"Later gorgeous...later."

CHAPTER TWELVE

As they left the bookstore, Gunner spotted the white envelope lying on the floor. He casually leaned over and shoved it into his pocket, never letting Darby know that another note was left. An hour later they were seated at his favorite diner finishing their breakfast.

Gunner smiled as his girls giggled while eating their pancakes. They both looked so damned beautiful it made his heart stop. Darby had emerged from her shower in a pair of white shorts, a turquoise halter top that showcased her assets a little too well, and those beautiful eyes...no makeup...just those gorgeous eyes staring at him.

Sweet Calla insisted on a dress so she could look pretty for uncle Tango. The little blue flowered sundress and matching sandals were adorable. Gunner watched her twirling, her long beautiful brown hair swinging behind her, and knew now how parents could get addicted to shoving their kids in pageants and talent shows. This kid belonged on a billboard, although he'd never let that happen...if it were his kid anyway.

"You still with us," smiled Darby.

"Yea gorgeous...all the way with you," he smiled.

"Gunner...do you always know the right thing to say? The right thing to do?" she asked.

"No...in fact rarely," he laughed. "But you two seem to bring out the best in me. I can't seem to not say the right thing around you two. My two beautiful girls."

"Mister Gunner," said Calla opening her backpack, "I have a present for you."

"For me?" he said looking shocked. She handed him a picture and Darby could tell he was choked up by it.

"That's you with the cape flying through the air and me and mommy are down here waving at you. Uncle Tango is over there watching for bad guys. You're my superhero Mister Gunner." He nodded, swallowing several times.

"It's the most perfect picture I've ever seen in my life," he said pulling Calla in for a hug. "I love you sweet girl...thank you."

"I love you too Mister Gunner." Darby felt the tears in her eyes as she watched her daughter give her unconditional love to this man, she'd barely known a few days. Gunner grinned up at her and mouthed 'thank you.' He couldn't have endeared himself more.

"Okay Calla," said Darby wiping her eyes, "let's get washed so we can go to Gunner's house." Darby stood and placed a sweet kiss against his lips as she walked toward the restroom. Gunner immediately opened the envelope, a fierce expression overcoming the previous one of joy. He took a quick snapshot of the note and sent it to Ace, who instantly called.

"Is this another one?" he asked Gunner.

"Yea. Asshole is getting more aggressive."

"I'll check the camera footage and hopefully have something for you when you get here."

"Make sure I'm alone Ace...don't do it in front of Darby and Calla," he said quietly.

"Sure thing." Ace hung up and Gunner plastered a smile on his face as the girls walked toward him. He left a few bills on the table and headed back out to his SUV. The girls were excited to see his house, but more so to meet his friends.

As Gunner pulled into the lot, Calla looked like she was in wonderland. Jumping from the SUV she grabbed her backpack and followed Gunner and Darby into the restaurant. Technically it was closed today, but their team and family would be allowed in and out. Gunner looked up to see almost everyone in the room, but only one person mattered to Calla. She took off running toward Tango, a big grin spread across his face.

"Uncle Tango!" she yelled. The entire team laughed as the big man picked her up spinning her around. She hugged his neck and kissed his cheek, making him blush. "I made something for you!"

"What?" he said acting shocked. "You made something for me?" She nodded smiling. Reaching into her backpack she pulled out the picture. There was a picture of a huge man with a big T on his shirt, in front of him was a little girl. Tango swallowed hard, looking up at the little girl.

"That's you uncle Tango...with the big T on your shirt. T is for Tango. You're watching over me like an uncle should do...see that's me...I'm safe cuz you're watching me." Tango nodded again and a few of the other men turned away, swallowing hard.

"It's the most beautiful picture ever Calla. I'm going to frame it and put it in my house." She hugged him again and then he turned her toward the others. "Everyone, this is Calla Greer, the daughter of that beautiful creature with Gunner."

"Hi, I'm Darby," she said blushing. There was a chorus of 'hellos' and Gunner growled when one of the twins let out a cat call whistle.

"Knock that off," said George walking toward them. "I'm George you beautiful little thing."

"Hello George," she said shaking his hand. George knelt down in front of Calla.

"Hello princess...my name is George."

"Like Prince George!" yelled Calla.

"Yes," he said seriously, "just like Prince George. Now...I could sure use some help with bakin' some cookies. Do you know anyone who might be able to help me with that?"

"Me...me!" she yelled excitedly.

"George are you sure? She can be a handful," said Darby.

"Honey, look around you. I keep all these folks fed and in line every day of the week, all year long. I think I can handle one little four-year-old princess." He held out a big leathery hand to Calla who slipped her hand in his and walked off toward the kitchen.

Gunner smiled at the two of them and then turned to look at his teammates.

"Officially, everyone this is Darby Greer...my girl," he said confidently.

"I knew it!" yelled a very pregnant woman. Darby looked over and saw the most beautiful woman she'd ever seen in her life and quite possibly the most pregnant woman she'd ever seen in her life. "I knew you had a girl!"

"Hello Darby," said Zulu. "That lovely woman with the very loud voice is my wife, Gabrielle or we all call her Angel eyes."

"I can see why, you're stunning," she said to the woman.

"Awww...I like her Gunner, don't screw it up," said Gabi. Gunner rolled his eyes and then turned Darby to the others.

"Darby this is Ghost, his wife Grace and their son JT; Doc and Bree, Whiskey and Kat, the twins Eagle and Hawk..."

"I love older women," said Hawk.

"I'm not sure that's a compliment," said Darby eyeing the younger man. "You need to work on your lines...but for future reference...I'm taken." Gunner laughed, pulling her close.

"Over there of course is Tango, Razor, Ice, and Axe. Skull is back there by the food," he grinned, "and..."

"And I'm Ace," said a very handsome man standing a few feet away from Darby.

"Well...I hope I don't have to remember that, but hello everyone. Thank you for inviting me and Calla today."

"She's beautiful Darby," said Grace.

"Thank you but she's also a handful as you can tell. She's already decided that 'uncle' Tango belongs to her."

"No need to worry about that beautiful," said Tango, "she's the only girl I do belong to." Darby nodded as they sat with Gunner's teammates chatting. An hour later, Calla appeared from the kitchen with George, both laughing and covered in flour.

"Oh, sweet Jesus," whispered Darby. "George I'm so sorry."

"Don't you dare say you're sorry," he laughed. "That was the most fun I've had in the kitchen in thirty years. I want her here all the time with me. Go ahead honey...give your present."

She held the plate very carefully in her hand, as if there were millions of dollars in jewels on it. She walked slowly to Tango, who already knew what was coming. He smiled as the others watched the little girl.

"It's for you uncle Tango...my first oatbeel raisin cookie."

"Oatmeal honey," said George grinning.

"Right...I get that wrong all the time...oatmeal." Tango took the plate and prepared himself for the cookie under the napkin. He peeled back the cloth and smiled. It looked like an ordinary, huge oatmeal raisin cookie. He picked it up and carefully took a bite, moaning as he did.

"Thought it was gonna be bad, didn't you?" asked Darby grinning. "She used to cook with her grandmothers' chef. She's quite the little chef herself."

"That is the best cookie I have EVER had," said Tango pulling her in for a hug.

"I love you uncle Tango," she whispered.

"I love you too kid," he said kissing her cheek.

"Hey...Mister Gunner...if all these are your brothers that means they're all my uncles right...and the ladies are my aunts."

"Uhhh...yea...I guess that's right," he said grinning.

"Awesome...I have uncles in all different colors...that's the best! Let's go uncle George." George grabbed her hand smiling and off they went. Eagle looked at all of them smiling.

"Damn...now that's a kid!"

CHAPTER THIRTEEN

While Darby casually chatted with the other women, Gunner excused himself to find Ace. Following close behind was Tango and Razor.

"What did you find?" asked Gunner.

"The drop off of the envelope was easy to find. Guy did nothing to hide himself, maybe he doesn't know we put up cameras. You can't really see his face, but appears to be about six foot, not very heavy, work boots...work pants...almost like a road crew worker. Might be black or Hispanic, I can't tell." Ace pointed to the screen as he explained and then turned.

"Okay, so we know he's dropping off in the middle of the night," said Tango.

"Maybe not," said Ace. "I went back to review the footage from earlier in the day. You guys did a good job of angling the cameras. I see him here...here...and here." He rolled the footage, speeding it up to the points he marked and pointing.

"It looks like he was waiting for her to return after lunch, but you guys were with her. Then last night, you stayed Gunner. Tango left and he started to move closer to the store and then stopped, realizing you didn't leave with him."

"Fuck!" growled Gunner.

"I don't think he wants to just drop off the letters, I think he wants to scare the shit out of her."

"What about Olivia Runyon?" asked Gunner.

"She's still in Memphis and from all outward appearances, is not worried that her granddaughter is gone. She hosted a museum fundraiser two nights ago and attended a charity auction last night. I can find no funds going out to private investigators, nothing to indicate she's looking for them at all."

"Damn...that seems cold," said Razor. "I mean Darby said the woman wanted to control their lives and she leaves and the woman decides she wants nothing to do with them?"

"Yea...something isn't right there," said Gunner. "Who owned the building before Darby bought it?"

"I'm looking into that now. A real estate firm owned the lease on it, but I'm trying to find the actual business that was there. I don't remember anything being there before Darby, but then again, I didn't go into town much. You guys?" asked Ace.

"I honestly don't remember what was there," said Gunner.

"Me either," said Razor.

"She staying here tonight?" asked Ace. Gunner nodded. "I'll keep an eye on the cameras and send Ice and Axe down there...maybe camp out in the bookstore for the night."

"Sounds good," said Gunner, "thanks Ace."

"No problem...and Gunner? Darby is beautiful, but that kid...that kid is the shit." Gunner let out a huge laugh and nodded walking out of Ace's office.

Tango stopped Gunner in the hall.

"So, the first note said 'give me what's mine...you can't hide' and the second note said 'I will have what belongs to me or you'll die' is that right?"

"Yea brother. I can't think of anything other than the old woman wanting the granddaughter. Darby doesn't own anything at all. She sunk all her money into that bookstore. Her ex-husband is dead, so it's not him and she's not dated anyone since Calla's birth." Tango got wide-eyed, staring at his friend.

"Well, we'll figure this out man...I'm here for you and both those girls. Lucky son-of-a-bitch," he grinned.

"You don't have to tell me brother," he said walking through the steel door. "When she came into the gym, I thought I was going to lose my shit right there and then she turned around and walked out. If it wasn't for Zulu telling me to chase her down, I might have lost her for good."

"I know one thing, it seems contagious around here," grinned Tango. "Look at all these happy brothers...makes a man sick."

Gunner laughed at his friend nodding, but he knew Tango was joking. George and Calla came back out from the kitchen, George holding her tablet in his hand.

"What's wrong honey?" asked Gunner kneeling down to kiss her sad face.

"My tablet won't work," she sniffed.

"Hmmm...I'm not very good at this kind of stuff," said Gunner.

"I am," said Ace standing behind them. He opened and closed his hands at his sides, and then smiled down at the little girl. "Come sit here with me...I'll sit right here. Let me see your tablet."

Gunner watched his brother gently dealing with the little girl, knowing his insides were probably on fire having to be that close to a child or any human. His head was down over the tablet, his fingers moving quickly over the device. Calla, as if knowing he was different sat quietly watching him. He looked up once and she smiled at him, he returned the smile, shaking his head.

"There," he said handing it back to her. "It's all fixed now. Be careful around food, okay? Sometimes that gets into it and makes it not feel good...like when you eat too many cookies."

"Can I hug you uncle Ace?" she asked. Gunner started to step forward and take her hand, but Ace nodded, opening his arms. The little girl walked slowly into his arms and gently lay her hands on his shoulders, patting him softly, not giving him a death grip hug like she'd done with Tango. "Thank you, uncle Ace."

"You are so very welcome sweet girl," he said standing and returning to his office.

"Well, I'll be damned," murmured Ghost, "she's the specops whisperer."

CHAPTER FOURTEEN

"I don't understand," said Darby watching her daughter hug another 'uncle'. The others were watching it as if it were a miracle that this man would hug a little girl.

"I'll explain later beautiful," said Gunner kissing her cheek. "How are you doing? Everything going okay over here?"

"Everything is great Gunner...thank you for inviting me and introducing me to your friends. They're all so wonderful...the women...the women are just amazing! I mean Grace is just out of this world, and Bree and Gabi doctors...Kat a ballerina and lawyer! I feel like a complete underachiever in this group."

"Baby you are no such thing...you are beautiful, intelligent, a business owner...a mom! You are the absolute most amazing woman I've ever met," he said kissing her. Darby saw that everyone was starting to move outside and stood, holding out her hand to Gunner.

"You know...the way Calla is running around here she'll wear herself out and sleep like the dead tonight." Gunner nodded and then understanding hit him and he smiled. "That's it handsome...stay with me. This morning...this morning Gunner was the most amazing experience of my life. I want more of those with you Gunner…a lot more and it scares me."

"I know it does gorgeous, but here's the thing…this morning was the most amazing thing ever for me too. You are the only woman that I have ever wanted to invite to my home Darby…ever. I have never wanted a woman to wake up in my bed…ever. I have never thought of myself as having a wife and child…ever. You walked into my club a few days ago and all that changed."

"I've sat here for the last year watching my teammates find their wives and wondered how they did it…how did it happen so fast for them. Then you walked in and I knew…I just fucking knew that you were the only woman for me. I know you're scared Darby…I know this scares you…but I am here for you for the long haul. I don't want anyone else…I don't want to be with anyone else." Darby let a tear slide down her cheek and Gunner kissed it away.

"We're a package deal Gunner…you know that," she whispered.

"Honey I am well aware of that. I know this is moving fast for you Darby, but I want you two in my life. When you're ready…when we're ready I want to be a family, Darby. I want you as my wife and I want that little girl to have my last name. I want there to be a Darby Michaels and Calla Michaels in my life."

"Oh God, Gunner...you can't just say things like that and not expect me to fall into your arms...that's not fair," she gasped. Gunner chuckled, pulling her in for a hug and kissing her sweet face.

"Mean every word of it baby...now let's go outside and enjoy this beautiful day. Get a feel for what it's' like being part of this fucked up family. Because mark my words beautiful, you will be part of this family sooner rather than later." He started to walk toward the door when Darby pulled him back. She looked like she wanted to say something, chewing on her bottom lip.

"I...Gunner...I think I love you," she whispered.

"Say it again," he smiled.

"I think I love you," she said again.

"That's damn good to hear gorgeous, because I know for a fucking fact, I love you and that little girl in there bathing in flour," he laughed. Darby nodded, kissing him again.

"How...how does this..." Gunner shook his head.

"Best not to question it honey. Just know it's not so unusual with my brothers, so I know it's damned sure possible. I love you and you love me. The rest will be easy."

Darby's head was literally spinning with the speed at which everything was happening, but every time she tried to tell herself to slow down, back up and take it easy, her stomach became unsettled and she knew that what was happening with her and Gunner was special.

She never had these feelings for Clint. She was definitely infatuated with him, attracted to him physically, but the thing that was missing that day in front of the minister, was love...a feeling that she would be incomplete without him. Somehow, Darby knew from the moment she laid eyes on Gunner that it was different. She knew that this man would make her feel whole...complete.

Sitting on the back porch watching the twins chase Calla around, Darby felt a sense of belonging she'd yearned for her entire life. At just nine years old, her parents left her with her aunt and uncle, saying they wanted to see the world while they were young. For Darby, it was a blessing in disguise. The hugs and kisses she'd craved as a little girl, were suddenly in abundance with her elderly aunt and uncle. Technically, they were her great aunt and great uncle, but it didn't matter to her.

They had no children of their own and doted on Darby for the remainder of their lives, giving her a life she could have only dreamed of before. After college graduation, she learned that her parents had divorced somewhere in Europe, her mother marrying a Turkish rug merchant and her father living in Prague somewhere. Neither ever contacted her again, never bothered to come home. A year before she met Clint, her aunt and uncle died within a few months of each other.

Maybe, she thought, maybe that's why she reached for Clint. Something that at least on the outside appeared to be strong...strong to hold onto. It turned out he was weak, but she'd found her own strength and her own voice in this.

Watching Gabi rub her belly, she smiled remembering that feeling.

"Are you due soon?" asked Darby.

"I wish," she grinned. "I'm having twins...monster sized twins thanks to that huge hunk of sexy chocolate on a stick."

"Ewwww...." Said Razor. "I haven't had my lunch...please."

"Oh Razor, you know he's a big sexy thing," winked Gabi.

"Zulu!" yelled Razor walking toward the big man at the horseshoe pits. "Your wife is making me sick again." Zulu laughed, blowing his wife a kiss. Darby could only laugh at their banter.

"Twins...that's really amazing," said Darby. Gabi nodded and told Darby the story of Grace and her twin daughters who were killed by her ex-husband. Seems all the women had stories that Darby needed to hear; stories that helped her understand what type of men were in this group.

By mid-afternoon the grounds were crowded with people and the grills were working overtime feeding the masses. Darby saw the woman who'd approached her and Gunner that day on the sidewalk, her pathetically thin body, fake breasts perched on her ribcage, curled into a man she assumed was her husband. Gunner held Darby close to his side, kissing her and she couldn't help but notice the woman's cold hard stare.

"Your friend doesn't like me very much," said Darby smiling up at him. Gunner looked down at her and then around the lawn shaking his head.

"That woman will never get it. She starves herself to death thinking it makes her more attractive to a husband that already seems to love her, and yet she constantly wants to prove her value and attractiveness by coming on to other men...I don't get it."

"I do...I mean...I understand," said Darby quietly. Gunner frowned at her. "Listen Gunner...women are all insecure about their bodies in some way. Breasts too big, too small; too heavy, too thin; too short, too tall; it's always something. Most of us don't understand that a man who is truly in love with a woman, loves her body no matter...or at least for the most part. I mean every man has his type...but women don't understand that. We are fed these images of what we should look like...images, which by the way are all the same, tall, thin, long hair, fake breasts, big lips; and when we're approached by a man who appears to be physical perfection..." she waved her hand up and down his body, "...we're intimidated and feel unworthy."

"Do you feel unworthy baby?" he frowned.

"No...yes...maybe," she said smiling up at him. "I know I'm not the ugliest girl in the room, but I also know I'm not Gabi...I mean...wowza! But...I also understand that Gabi isn't every mans' cup of tea and neither am I. Some men are going to love the way I look, some will hate it. I'm confident enough to be okay with that, to move on if I'm not what you want. Some women aren't that confident. I suspect that she...Joan...is so unsure of herself, so unsure of what her husband wants she's grasping at straws and just looking for some sort of confirmation that she's still an attractive woman."

"That's some seriously insightful shit beautiful," said Gunner. "How did you gather all that?"

"One, I'm a woman and have felt that way in my past. Two, you can tell she's trying so hard for perfection, not even sure what that looks like. And three, I've been watching her husband holding onto her arm, not her hand, like she's a trophy...while he flirts, hugs, kisses, and leers at every woman who walks by him." Gunner immediately looked up watching Joan's husband for a few minutes.

"We might need to escort him off property," said Razor frowning in the direction of Joan and her husband.

"Keep an eye on him," said Gunner. "If he touches one woman inappropriately ask him to leave. I think we should have Bree talk to Joan on Monday at the gym."

"See," smiled Darby leaning up to kiss him, "you're the most amazing man ever...that's why I love you."

"Love you my gorgeous girl...now let me go wear out the little one so she'll be conked out tonight...I've got plans."

CHAPTER FIFTEEN

"Where is my package and my money?" The other man shifted nervously from one foot to another, staring down at his feet and then up to face the man seated in front of him. He wasn't really nervous at all. In this equation, he held all the markers, but he wanted him to believe he was in charge.

"It's not that simple, sir."

"Explain to me why it's not that simple. My money and my package were left in that building and that woman knows something about it."

"Sir, I don't think she does. She bought the building from the real estate agent; she had no knowledge of the tenant before. She wasn't even a resident here before she arrived. I don't think she has a clue what's in the building."

"And I don't give a damn," he said standing to stare the man directly in the eyes. "I want my package and money. It's in that building. Kill her and get me what I'm owed."

"Sir, as I said it's not that simple. She has security...cameras, sensors, everything. This motorcycle club is hanging out there now. I don't think it's going to be that easy."

He looked up at the man in front of him and clenched his jaw, his frustration more than evident with the man. Walking around his desk he paced behind the man, rubbing his temples in vain trying to rid himself of the headache he felt coming on.

"A motorcycle club?" he asked.

"Yes sir," he replied quickly. "These guys don't screw around. The stuff they put up is top of the line and they definitely aren't going to let us just walk in there and take over."

"That should tell you that she knows what she has in that building. I want it...all of it. It's mine, owed to me by that idiot Haslett. He neglected to tell me he was dying so I had no way to ask him what he did with everything before he left. He has no children, no wife...nothing!"

"But do you know what he does have?" he asked the other man.

"No sir."

"Of course, you don't because it's not important to you...it's my fucking product and my fucking money! Except I'm going to make this important to you. Take the child...find a way to kidnap the child and get the woman to give you, my stuff."

"Sir...I'm telling you she knows nothing about this. I just have to get in the building and then I can get you your money and product. Taking that kid will not end well for you. That club isn't normal."

"What do you mean they're not normal? They're a bunch of leather wearing, motorcycle riding hoodlums, that's all they are!" The man blew out a breath and braced himself.

"Sir, they are the Steel Patriots. They own several legitimate businesses and they were formed from a core group of Special Forces operatives. These guys are not normal motorcyclists and from what I can tell, one of them is dating the woman. If we mess with her or that child, we're going to be biting off more than we can chew...way more."

He paced the room once more like a lion in a cage. If these men were what he said, he needed to back up just a bit and formulate a different plan. The last thing he needed was a bunch of ex-military snooping in his business.

"Alright...we do it your way for now. Find a way to get into her business...be a frequent book club member for all I care. She didn't do any renovations so it's either in the store itself or the apartment. Tear it apart for if that's what it takes, but make it happen."

"Yes sir," he said leaving the room. Two other men stood by the truck waiting for him as he exited the building. "Let's go...we need to rip that place apart."

CHAPTER SIXTEEN

Gunner and Darby bid their goodnights to the rest of the team and walked the path toward his home. It was a warm summer night, but the cooler mountain breezes kept it from being stifling.

"You have someone to cover the bookstore tomorrow babe?" he asked as they opened the door to his house. Calla was sound asleep on his shoulder, long since passed out.

"I do," she smiled pushing her daughters' hair from her face. "One the college girls I hired; Amanda is going to take the afternoon shift for me. I'm only open noon to four on Sundays and she needs the hours."

"Good," he said smiling down at her, he pressed a quick kiss to her lips and then stood up again. "I have plans with my girls tomorrow." Gunner walked down a long hallway and turned the bedside table lamp on, smiling. This was exactly the way he'd dreamed it would be. His girls, in his home...their home...with Calla sleeping in this room.

Laying her on the bed, he carefully removed her shoes and then her mother removed her dress. Slipping her between the covers, they both kissed her forehead and turned off the light.

"She'll sleep late tomorrow," whispered Darby. "I can't believe how good the twins and Ace were with her. I mean I know they're all fairly young, but wow, those guys are top notch babysitters."

"Well, it was a shock to watch Ace connect with her. Brother's had it bad in his life and to see him connect to someone, even a kid, was pretty fucking incredible. And as for Calla sleeping late? I'm thrilled to hear that baby, because I have plans for you tonight," he said pulling her into his body. He walked in the other direction toward his bedroom and flipped on the light. He was grateful he'd cleaned the night before and smiled as Darby looked around the room.

"It's a beautiful house Gunner," she said grinning.

"Thank you. We all built homes here as we felt the need for more privacy. Some of the guys, the twins and a few others, still live in the barn."

"I can see the advantage of all of you being close if someone needs anything. It's like your own little community." He nodded, watching as she nervously walked around the room.

"Nothing to be nervous about beautiful. I saw that body this morning and I want to see more of it, taste more of it." She blushed and nodded once again. "Okay what's going on in that head of yours, sweetheart?"

"Nothing...I mean...it's silly. I know you saw some of me this morning, but...I've had a baby Gunner. I'm not the woman with the flat stomach or the perky breasts."

"No, you're not thank fuck! I don't want that woman Darby...I want a real woman...I want you. That little tummy you have is sexy as hell. It tells me that you gave life to that gorgeous little thing down the hall. Those beautiful legs of yours tell me that you don't mind a little hard work. And your tits? Baby...those beauties make me want to embarrass myself in my jeans."

"Oh wow," she whispered, "you really do know what to say." He chuckled and pulled his t-shirt over his head.

"I smell like the barbecue...care to shower with me?" he asked grinning at her. She nodded nervously, following him into the huge bathroom. There was a massive stand-alone tub on one end and a shower big enough for an entire family, with seating all around the edges.

"Wow…I'm having serious bathroom envy right now," she said looking around. Gunner laughed, pulling her toward him, gently untying her halter top. He released the ties and her breasts exhaled, free at last.

"No need to have envy baby…it's yours now too." Darby unzipped her shorts and shoved them down her tanned legs, the scrap of thong gone with them. She stood, fully naked in front of Gunner and all she heard was a rumbling growl.

"Fucking hell woman," he said staring at her. "You are so damned beautiful Darby…and you're mine." She unzipped his shorts and shoved them to his ankles smiling.

"And you're mine Gunner Michaels and I'm so very glad you chased me out of that gym." She said the last word against his lips as he lifted her and settled them beneath the steamy, hot spray of water. Gunner took the soap and delicately washed her body as her tiny hand gripped his cock, stroking up and down. He was about to embarrass himself, when he pushed her down to the stone seat, spreading her legs wide.

Kneeling before her, he let his tongue dance across her beautiful sweet pussy, gliding in and out as her breath came faster and faster.

Darby gripped his head, holding him against her as she writhed against his lush lips.

"Gunner...oh...oh Gunner..." she moaned. He smiled up at her as she moaned in sweet release against his mouth.

"Now you're ready for me baby," he said grinning at her. He pulled the towels from the shelf and wrapped them both up, walking her to the bed. "This is where I wanted you...needed you this morning. Open for me beautiful." Darby did as he asked and spread her knees wide, watching Gunner flush with desire.

"Fuck me you're beautiful," he said against her lips. His cock touched her opening and she gasped, looking down.

"Damn...I think you're bigger than you were this morning." Gunner chuckled, shaking his head.

"No baby...you just aren't in a rush now...get a good look love...it's all yours," he said teasing her wet entrance with his big purple head. Darby moaned at the sight of it, opening wider, inviting him inside and he gladly took the invitation sinking his length inside her hot tight pussy.

"Oh...wow...," murmured Darby.

"Yea baby…wow…you're so fucking beautiful Darby…so perfect for me baby. I'm so damned lucky," he said pulling out and sinking all the way back inside her once again.

"Gunner…oh fuck honey…faster," she cried scratching her nails across his back. Gunner broke out in goosebumps, the feel of her nails raking him with lust and need. Nodding, he moved faster and faster insider her. When Darby wrapped her legs around his hips and squeezed Gunner nearly screamed with his release. He felt the hot spurts of cum filling her hole and she shook with satisfaction.

As he slowed, she moved again, rocking against him. She clenched the walls of her pussy around his cock, squeezing the last of his juices out and priming him for the next round.

"Fuck baby…yea squeeze me like that…" Darby took control and rolled, flipping on top of Gunner, straddling his hips. His cock never left the warmth of her sweet hole and when she started bucking against him like a rodeo queen, it was all he could do not to reach up and roughly squeeze her tits.

As usual, Darby surprised him, grabbing his hands, she placed them on her breasts and tightened around them.

"Squeeze me Gunner...suck my nipples...make me cum," she moaned.

"Gladly baby," he smiled gripping her tits hard, twisting the big sensitive nipples. "Fuck yea gorgeous...fucking love these." Darby arched her back moaning with desire, driving harder against his hot stick. When he bit down on her nipple, she screamed her release and he was right behind her. Their bodies so in sync it was as if their orgasms were connected by an invisible thread.

Gunner's body was covered in his own sweat, but also Darby's as she lay on top of him, their breathing in time with one another. He shoved back the straight black hair from her face and kissed her, rolling her to his side and enveloping her in his big arms.

"Shit that was good," he smiled.

"It was good," she grinned. "You're very, very good at this Gunner."

"Baby don't discount your part in this. I'm only as good as my partner and you gorgeous are the most amazing fucking woman ever. I'm not a choir boy Darby, I won't lie to you about my past, but I've never felt this way about a woman and I damned sure have never had an orgasm like that with a woman before. You're it baby…plain and simple…you're it."

"Me too Gunner…I only had a few other partners before Clint, and you know he was the last. He wasn't anything to write home about," she grinned. "I think I did what a lot of women do and judged the outer package on what he was going to be like in the bedroom. It was really disappointing. You…you are anything but a disappointment."

"Makes me fucking happy to hear that beautiful, because if I were a disappointment, we'd just have to practice until we got it right." Darby smiled up at him and nodded.

"Well…I didn't say we were perfect…I mean practice makes…" Before she could finish her sentence, his mouth was on hers, his cock already buried inside her once again.

CHAPTER SEVENTEEN

Ice and Axe watched the cameras from their tablets in the truck, keeping one eye on the building, the other on the tablets. Main Street was dark in their little town, most businesses rolling up the carpet at around ten. The retail shops typically closed by five, the restaurants closing around nine or ten. It was the only tough part about being here as a single guy, if you wanted a late-night drink you had to go three towns over to stay up until midnight. Most nights they just hung out at Club Steel.

"That kid sure is cute, isn't she?" said Axe referring to Calla.

"Yea man...and her mama isn't half bad either...don't tell Gunner I said that," he grinned. "She's just really, classically beautiful you know?" Axe nodded at his friend smiling.

"Yea, I know what you mean. All the women are great. You ever think of settling down?" asked Axe.

"I don't know...six months ago I would have said hell no. Now? It doesn't seem like such a bad idea. I'm coming up on thirty and I know you are too. No offense to Ghost, but I don't want to be forty-five popping out my first kid knowing I'll be getting social security when they graduate high school. I want to be young enough to throw a ball, or hell coach ball." Ice shook his head, lost in thought.

"I hear ya. I sometimes wonder how those lucky bastards got Grace, Bree, Kat, and Gabi...and now Darby, I guess. Feels like the love fairy dropped their gorgeous ass's right in their laps. I mean...I know that's not what happened. What happened to Grace was terrible and Bree, shit what she had to go through was almost as bad."

"I know what you mean brother. I guess we just have to start putting ourselves out there more," he said grinning at him. Ice looked up and down the street letting out a long slow breath.

"Nobody fucking here man," said Ice.

"Yea I know...but something doesn't feel right. I've seen that black truck drive by like three times now. I didn't think anything at first, but it keeps slowing down."

"You think we should drive away? Make them think we're gone?" asked Ice.

"Yea...just do a circle, come back around and park in the back." Axe watched the truck slow down as they pulled away and looking in his rear-view mirror, it was exactly what he thought would happen, the truck slowed down and parked.

Ice parked the truck in the back parking lot where a few other cars remained from the evening. Keeping his screen on his phone open, he watched as three men exited the vehicle in front of the store, making their way to the front door. One looked straight up into the camera, his buddy smacking him on the back of the head as if to warn him.

Axe grinned, knowing that Ace would get that face on camera and they could run facial recognition. The three men tried the door and then noticing the keypad, stepped back talking to one another.

"Should we go around front and take them?" asked Ice.

"No…nothing to take them down for yet. Let them snoop and we'll keep an eye out." The men stood in front of the store for nearly twenty minutes just talking and then just as suddenly, got back in the truck and left.

"Think they'll be back?"

"Not sure, but let's go ahead and get inside. Darby said we could sleep upstairs tonight. We'll hear anything if they try to break in." Axe and Ice entered the code, looking up to give a wave to Ace, who they were sure was watching. Locking themselves in the store, they made their way up to the apartment.

Axe took the sofa, while Ice took Darby's bed. Both men lay awake, listening to the sounds of the old building creaking with every breeze.

"You asleep in there?" asked Axe.

"Fuck no," said Ice. "Wonder if Darby has any beer?"

"One way to find out…" Opening the refrigerator he smiled taking out a couple of beers. "A game of cards?" Axe nodded as the men sat on the floor playing poker for several hours. Sometime around three, they both crashed. When Ice woke and looked up at the clock, it was nearly ten-thirty. Looking down at his phone there was only one message from Ace. He was taking the system offline for a few hours since it was daylight, but not to worry, he would have it back up by five.

Ice stood and went to the bathroom to relive himself. Rubbing his hand over his face, he splashed some cold water on himself and went in search of coffee. Axe stirred in the other room and he realized there was a coffee shop right next door that probably had food as well.

Ice locked the apartment door and walked downstairs toward the book shop. Stepping out he heard a small noise at the back of the store. Gripping his Glock in his hand, he maneuvered around the shelves and swung toward the sound. He was greeted by a terrified face...a beautiful, young, bright-eyed, terrified face.

"Holy fuck," he whispered. "Who are you?"

"A-Amanda...I-I work here...f-for Darby," she stuttered.

"Shit! I'm sorry," he said holstering his gun. "I thought you were a robber. I'm a friend of Darby's, I work with her boyfriend Gunner."

"She has a boyfriend?" asked the girl.

"It's new," he grinned. "Sorry I scared you. I'm Ice...I mean my name is Decker McManus, but they call me Ice."

"Amanda Nettles. I'm working here in between semesters," she said staring him up and down.

"Huh? College? I would have thought high school," he said more to himself than to the girl.

"Thanks...I think. I'm actually headed into my last semester at UVA. I'm twenty-one." He nodded thoughtfully and then realized he was staring at the girl. In his defense, she was beautiful. She had long brown hair, with natural highlights sprinkled throughout, her pretty hazel eyes had flecks of green and yellow. The short little dress did nothing to conceal her long, lean legs. Her small breasts resting on delicately soft skin.

"Uh...well I was going next door to get coffee. You want some?"

"Oh...yea sure if you don't mind."

"Don't mind at all Sorority," he smiled. She looked up frowning at him and then looked down at her dress. She knew she wasn't like some of the other girls, coming from rich elitist families, driving daddy's new sports car, and buying clothes like she bought groceries. She was backwoods poor and it showed in the second-hand clothes she wore and tried to pass off as 'vintage'.

"I'm not in a sorority and I don't plan to be. My name is Amanda, please use it." She turned and set a stack of books on the counter, her back to Ice, tears threatening to spill.

"Hey...hey I'm sorry...shit, I'm really sorry. I didn't mean it as an insult. I mean you look like a sorority girl, all beautiful and pure and innocent."

"Huh, you don't know much about sorority girls, do you?" she said with a sneer.

Okay...pretty girl doesn't like sororities...noted.

"I'm really sorry and you're right, I don't know anything about sorority girls. I went to school online while in the Navy. Coffee?"

"Sure...black, no sugar, one cream." She'd surprised him once again with her order and he turned to head next door.

"Oh, by the way, my buddy is upstairs as well. His name is Axe...Axel Mains. If you hear footsteps just let him know you're here." She nodded and watched as he left the store. A few minutes later he was back with the coffee and a box of pastries. He texted his friend who came down a few minutes later. Amanda couldn't help but notice how good looking both men were.

Their hair was slightly longer than she liked on a guy, but they were all man. Both had tattoos up and down their arms, one had crystal clear blue eyes, the other deep rich brown eyes, but it was the one named Ice that set her blood on fire.

Slow down girl...one more semester and you're out of this hell...no distractions.

"Well," said Ice, "since you're here now, we'll head out. Darby should be back this evening. If you run into any problems before then, just give me a call." He handed a piece of paper with his number on it and smiled at her. She nodded, gracing him with just the hint of a grin, but it was enough for Ice.

As they headed to the barn, Axe grinned at his friend.

"Cute girl," he said.

"Yea...girl...not woman, girl."

"Brother, I think you've lost your fucking mind. She said she was twenty-one, a senior in college, more than legal and that damned sure was no girl...she was woman all the way." Ice cursed under his breath...not because he was angry...because he had no reply to that logic.

CHAPTER EIGHTEEN

Darby woke, stretching her body to discover delightful places she was aching. She rolled over to find a cold empty bed, her heart dropping to her stomach. *Get it together Darby...you're in his damned house...he wouldn't leave his own house.* She pushed from the bed, stretching and pulled on a clean pair of shorts and t-shirt. Quickly brushing her teeth, she splashed her face with cold water and opened the bedroom door...then smiled.

The sounds of laughter floated upstairs, her daughters' giggles mixed with the smell of coffee and something else. She walked slowly so as not to disturb the moment, taking one step at a time. As she rounded the corner, she heard the conversation, tucking herself back around the wall.

"Were you always this big Mister Gunner?" asked Calla.

"Me? No way! I was so little my mom and dad had to give me special food to help me grow." She could see her daughters' wide eyes and heard her gasp. "Yep...my older brother was really big and always protected me in school until I got bigger."

"Wow...you have a brother?" she asked.

"I do. I have two in fact, both younger than me. Keep stirring," he said pointing to the bowl.

"What are their names?"

"Hunter and Striker."

"Uncle Hunter and uncle Striker," she whispered. Gunner grinned at the little girl and nodded.

"Gunner...I mean Mister Gunner..."

"You can just call me Gunner baby, it's okay."

"Ummm...okay...Gunner...did you have a daddy?" she asked. Gunner stopped what he was doing and looked at the little girl perched on his kitchen counter. Her long brown hair was pushed back in a messy ponytail that he'd tried to tie for her. She had dressed herself in her shorts and top, her feet bare, dangling from the counter.

"I do have a daddy, he's still alive. He was the best dad in the whole world," he said smiling.

"He...he didn't hit you or yell at you? Did you get to see him every day?" asked Calla.

"No baby, he didn't hit me or yell at me. He had rules and we had to follow the rules, but they were to make sure that my brothers and I were safe. He used to take us to baseball games and to the movies...he even took us camping and fishing." Calla nodded, looking down at her feet.

Darby gripped her chest, wanting to sob for the loss her daughter was feeling.

"I wish I had a daddy like that," she said quietly. Gunner lifted the girl from the counter, carrying her to the kitchen table, where he sat her in front of him on top of the table.

"You listen to me sweet Calla. You are the most beautiful, lovable little girl in the whole world. One day…soon I hope…I'm going to ask your mommy to marry me and then I'm going to ask you to be my little girl…"

"Yes! I want to be your little girl," she cried wrapping her arms around his neck. Gunner chuckled and hugged her back.

"Well, now you have to hear the whole deal, okay?" Her little head nodded up and down. "You have to clean your room, make your bed, listen to your mom and me, go to school…"

"I do all that now," she said excitedly.

"I know baby girl, but you also have to be kind, love others, be sweet to your aunts and uncles, kind to the babies they're going to have. I also expect that you'll have to eat your vegetables." She frowned staring at him.

"I'm allergic to vegetables." Darby almost burst out laughing.

"Is that the truth or a tale?" asked Gunner seriously. She bit her lower lip and looked down.

"A t-tale...I just don't like anything green," she said. He nodded with a stern expression.

"Well...I'll be honest, I don't like some of the green stuff either. How about I see if we can make a deal with mom and only have green stuff three times a week." She held up two fingers and he shook his head. "No can-do kiddo...three times."

"Okay, if I eat my green stuff three times in a week, make my bed, clean my room, and mind the adults...will you be my daddy...will you make sure no one is mean to me ever again?" Gunner swallowed hard, pulling Calla into his big chest.

"Baby, even if for some rotten reason I don't become your daddy, I will make sure no one is ever mean to you again...I promise," he said kissing her forehead. Darby couldn't take it any longer, she turned the corner smiling at the two conspirators.

"Good morning," she said cheerfully.

"Morning beautiful," he said standing to kiss her. "We've been making breakfast."

"And just so you know mommy...Gunner is gonna be my daddy one day and then you can sleep with him all the time." Calla hopped down and took off toward the living room, turning on the cartoons once again. Darby could only stand there open-mouthed, then turned to see Gunner grinning.

"She is right baby. Marry me...let me wake up to you every morning...let me make that little girl mine. I know what you're thinking...I understand what you're feeling Darby, but I don't want to live without the two of you. I want to wake up every morning like I did today, with you curled up next to me and that little girl anxiously waiting for me to make breakfast with her."

"God Gunner," she said letting out a slow breath. "I...I want this I do..."

"Too fast?" he said smiling at her.

"A little," she grinned. "Give me a few days to think?" He nodded kissing her.

"Not going anywhere baby, but just so you know, neither are you."

CHAPTER NINETEEN

Ice and Axe smiled at the other brothers seated across from them, telling them of the three idiots who found themselves on camera last night. Ace was still trying to identify the one that looked up, but they were certain he would be in a database somewhere.

"So, the little fuckers thought they'd just walk right in and create mayhem?" asked Tango.

"Guess so," shrugged Ice. "Once they saw all the cameras and sensors they backed away. We slept in the apartment and didn't hear a thing until I came down this morning. Nearly scared the shit out of Darby's part-time help."

"Damn brother, try not to kill the help," grinned Tango.

"She was just a scared college kid," he said brushing it off. He didn't want to think about the little girl in the book store, although the more he thought about her, the more he recognized she wasn't a little girl.

"Anybody see the little hotties that came to the barbecue last night?" asked Razor grinning at the group.

"Which ones?" smiled Tango, although the one he wanted to show up hadn't.

"The four all dressed alike...cut offs so high you could see their ass cheeks, tiny little tank tops with no bra...fuck brother...that was some good-looking ass there."

"Yep," said Eagle, "tasted good too."

"You shithead," said Razor grinning, "Which one did you take to bed?"

"All of 'em," said Hawk and Eagle together. Tango looked up at the two men and back at Razor.

"You two little shits telling me you fucked four women...together last night?" asked Tango. Eagle just shrugged, but it was Hawk that gladly gave them the details.

"Chicks dig twins, brother. They all took their turns with us and each other...some next level freaky shit right there. They all work at some big clothing store in the city. Heard about Club Steel and wanted a taste of a biker."

"Taste indeed," said Eagle grinning at his twin. Tango groaned uncomfortably in his chair, fixing his dick as it hardened hearing about the twins and the four girls.

"One of 'em was even too freaky for me," said Hawk. "Shit, that little blonde with the curls? That bitch came prepared. She had cuffs, whips, even brought her own dildos. Didn't want to touch that shit, but she damned sure played with it on her friends."

"Fuuu..."

"Uncle Tango!"

"Fudge," he said quickly. "Hi precious...did you sleep good?"

"Yes! I just wanted to make sure you had a good sleep too," she said smiling. He laughed and pulled her onto his lap.

"I did, thank you. That's very sweet of you." She nodded her little head and looked around the room.

"Did you have a good sleep uncle Hawk? Uncle Eagle?" She went down the line and each man looked at her, knowing she was up to something.

"Okay squirt, we all had a good sleep. What's up with the questions?" asked Tango.

"Well...Gunner said if he and mommy get married and he's my dad I have to clean my room and make my bed and mind mommy and him, but he also said I have to be nice to everyone...to be sweet to the adults...so I'm tryin' real hard. But..."

"But what precious?" asked Tango.

"They're gonna make me eat my green stuff," she said with a disgusted face. Tango stood with her in his arms looking angry.

"What!? This is outrageous! Where are they?" Calla giggled as Tango took off down the hallway with her in search of her mom and Gunner. Ice could only smile at the sweet interaction, then feeling his phone vibrate, pulled it out of his pocket to see an unknown number.

"Hello?"

"Ummm...Ice...I mean...Decker, this is Amanda," she said in a whisper.

"Hey Amanda, what's up? Is everything okay?"

"I'm not sure…there are two guys in here and they've been here for like hours. I keep asking if they need help but they just glare at me and…they're making me really uncomfortable," she said quietly.

"Stay where you are sweetheart, we're on our way…stay on the line," he said silencing the phone. "Axe? Let's go…two dudes at the bookstore creeping Amanda out." Axe nodded as they headed toward their bikes.

"Decker…one of the guys just lifted up some floorboards…what do I do?" she said in a shaky voice.

"Nothing honey, just pretend like you don't see or hear anything okay…we're ten minutes away." He engaged the speaker on his bike and spoke softly to her the entire drive down the mountain. Parking the bikes a few blocks away, they took off in a jog toward the store. Axe took the rear exit, while Ice walked in the front door, casually.

"H-hi," said Amanda. Ice shook his head slightly and she nodded. "Can I help you find something?"

"Nope, just looking around, thanks." He said watching her. He waved at her to go out the front door and she nodded, headed out and toward the coffee shop. Ice pulled his Glock and looked down the first row of books, whistling a casual tune, softly as he did. He spotted Axe coming in the back door and nodded in the direction of the noise.

"Put the boards back," he heard the man whisper.

"Fuck off you put them back," said the other one. Ice turned the corner, seeing two men hovered over a large opening in the floor.

"I have an idea," he said pointing the weapon at them, "why don't you both put the boards back and then tell me what the fuck you're doing tearing up my friends' store?"

"Shit."

"Yea…shit is an accurate description of what you've gotten yourself into. Put the boards back." The two men nodded, replacing the boards. Two minutes later Ice heard the motorcycles out front and looked up to see Ghost, Tango, and Gunner.

Ghost walked in; his six-foot-four frame seemingly larger with his motorcycle boots. His long salt and pepper hair was tied in a top knot, his aviator sunglasses perched on his nose. Both of the men on the floor swallowed, looking up at the group walking in the door.

Behind Ghost was Tango – whose six-foot-three was nearly as big as Ghost, but Gunner's thick arms and broad chest made both of them sit back a bit.

"You little fuckers!" yelled Gunner. "Did you think you could tear up my womans' shop and get away with it?"

"Gunner? Let us handle this," said Tango quietly. "Where's the girl?"

"Sent her next door," said Ice. "I'll go sit with her and get whatever info she has." Tango nodded and then turned to the two men.

"Really shit the bed on this one boys. Why are you here?" he asked. Both men said nothing, still seated on the floor, their arms resting on their knees. Tango waited a few seconds, as patiently as he was able, then swung his long leg in a sweeping motion kicking both men in the side of the head.

"Let's start again...why...the fuck...are you here?"

"We don't know," said one of them rubbing the side of his face. "We were told to find a box that belonged to some old dude, that's all."

"What old dude?" asked Gunner.

"I don't know...seriously man...we don't know."

"Who do you call if you find the box?" asked Tango. He waited patiently as the men looked at one another and then back at the circle of giants standing in front of them. "I'm only going to ask my questions once asshole."

"We...we call this guy...Javier. If we find the shit, we call him and he comes and takes it from us."

"Call him," said Tango.

"Wh-what?" he stammered. "No...no fucking way man...the old dude will kill us."

"I'm going to kill you either way, but this way you get to choose whether it's fast or slow. Call the mother-fucker now!" yelled Tango.

Gunner stood back wanting to take a piece of their hide, but knew it was someone much bigger they really wanted. He could tell the two men were mulling over in their minds the best option.

"I'll call."

"We're dead if you do," said the other man.

"Shut up...you heard him...we're dead either way. Shit's not worth it to me." He looked up at Gunner and Tango. "My phone is in my back pocket."

"Stand up," said Gunner. The man stood and Gunner slammed him hard against the wall, his nose cracking, blood trailing down his face. "Ooops, sorry about that." He let the man pull out his phone hitting the number. Gunner grabbed it, setting it on speaker.

"Yea."

"We have the box," he said.

"What's wrong with your voice?" asked the other man.

"Allergies, fucking dust everywhere in this place."

"Whatever...I'm out of pocket until Tuesday. Hold it somewhere safe. Don't call anyone else, just wait for a call from me...you understand Corey?" The man rolled his eyes, fucking hell he'd just given them his name.

"Yea Javier, I understand." He ended the call and Gunner pocketed his phone.

"Javier...what's his last name?" asked Tango.

"Ascencio...Javier Ascencio. That's all I know man." Gunner nodded at Tango and Razor as they pulled the two men out the back door of the building.

"Don't worry brother, we'll find out what the shit is happening here," said Ghost. Gunner nodded looking at the hole in the floor. "What?"

"He said they had the 'box'; they're looking for a box of some sort. What if we found it first? I can see if Darby will let us close down the store for a few days, we could search everything, use some of our equipment to see if anything is in the walls." Ghost nodded.

"Do it."

CHAPTER TWENTY

Ice walked into the coffee shop and immediately noticed Amanda seated in the corner, her hands wrapped around a cup of coffee.

"Hey," he said sitting across from her, "you okay?" She nodded, then shook her head, tears filling her eyes. "It's okay honey...everything is going to be okay. You did the right thing calling me."

"I was so scared Decker...so scared. I'm tired of being scared...tired of always looking over my shoulder," she said wiping her tears away. Ice looked at her with concern on his face. What the fuck was she looking over her shoulder for? Who was she afraid of?

"No shame in being afraid honey, we all are sometimes."

"Even you?" she asked with a grin.

"Even me. If you aren't scared, you're not paying attention. It's a scary world, there's always something out there to be afraid of." She nodded, biting her lower lip. He was going to get to her fear in a minute, but first he had some questions.

"What happened with the two next door?" he asked.

"It's like I told you, they came in and just started wandering the aisles. I heard a knocking and walked back to where they were and one of them was knocking on the wall. When I asked if he needed something, he told me to leave him alone, they were just looking. Then a little while later is when I heard the creaking of the floor boards. When I peeked around the shelf, they were prying the boards loose. That's when I got really scared and called you."

"I'm glad you did honey," he said reaching for her hand, holding it between the warmth of his own.

"I-I should go back to the store," she said trying to pull her hand away.

"Not yet...let the boys have a conversation with those two. Gunner is on his way and he'll let us know what to do about the store."

"Damn! I can't afford to lose my job," she said crying once more.

"You won't lose your job honey, I promise. Even if Darby has to shut it down for a bit, the Steel Patriots will make sure you're paid. You could even help us out at Club Steel and maybe bartend or wait tables."

"Really?" she asked. Her eyes lit up with the prospect of having another job and something in Ice's gut told him this girl needed help.

Damn. Was it the way of the Patriot's to only find women who need help?

"Really," he smiled. "You have any experience?" She nodded quickly.

"Yea...I mean I've been working for Darby for about a month, since I got home for summer break. I wanted to finish out my semester this summer, but the classes I needed weren't available. But before that I worked at a little bar off campus in the evenings and a coffee shop in the mornings."

"You seem to be in a rush to finish school. That's a lot of jobs for one little girl," he smiled.

"I've already told you, I'm not a little girl and some of us need to work a lot of jobs to survive. I need to finish school so I can start working full-time. I need...I just need a full-time job with full-time pay." He eyed her cautiously and nodded again. Amanda felt her face heat up at his perusal of her body and she immediately started to sweat. Pushing her sleeves up on her sweater, she heard his sharp intake of breath and immediately realized her mistake.

"What the fuck?" he growled gripping her wrist, pulling her arm toward him. Amanda pushed the sleeves back down, but Decker pulled her arm toward him shoving it back up. "Who the fuck touched you like that?"

"It...it doesn't matter okay...please Decker...I just need this job," she said with a tear.

"Look at me Amanda...look at me honey. I'm not going to hurt you, but I'm damned sure not letting anyone put marks on you like that ever again. Now who the fuck touched you like that?"

"M-my stepfather."

"Has he..." She shook her head.

"Not for lack of trying," she sniffed. "Listen Decker, I can tell you're a good person, who has lived a good life. I have not. I come from trash...literally trailer park trash. My mother is a drunk and my stepfather is a brutal asshole who likes making me feel like shit and does everything in his power to knock me down a peg or two when he can. I knew I had to get out and so I did. I've put myself through school on scholarships and loans and I'm so close I can taste it. If I stay in that trailer too long...he's going to succeed. I can't fight him forever. I need this job."

"You're not safe there."

"Probably not," she said tilting her head sideways, "which is why I'm living out of my car for the most part. I go home to shower when I know he's at work and my mother is gone drinking with her friends. It's not a good choice, but then again, I don't really have a choice."

"Yea you do honey. You can stay with me." He said it so matter-of-factly she thought she hadn't heard him right.

"Decker...I don't even know you. I met you this morning while at the other end of your pistol! I hardly think that's the beginning of a positive relationship!" Decker grinned at her and nodded.

"I know it might feel that way, but I can offer you a safe place to live, no one hitting you, no one bothering you. The barn portion of the club has suites where a lot of the single guys stay. We have guest rooms for people we help. You would have your own room, own bathroom and a small living room...rent free. You can work at the bar or here at the bookstore and when the summer is up, you finish school free from worry."

"I'm not sleeping with you," she said crossing her arms over her chest.

"I didn't ask." He grinned at her, watching her turn bright red, then turning from him, biting that beautiful lower lip. "Don't think for a moment I won't ask honey, but for now, let me at least get you safe."

"Why? Why would you do this for someone you don't even know?" she asked. He shrugged looking at her beautiful hazel eyes.

"Because it's what we do honey...we save the world."

"Must be exhausting," she muttered.

"You have no idea."

CHAPTER TWENTY-ONE

"So let me see if I have this straight," said Darby crossing her arms and staring at Gunner, Tango, and Ice. "Someone tried to tear up my store and Amanda called Ice to stop them. You guys took off, stopped them from tearing it up…thank you…and now want to do it yourselves. Amanda meanwhile, is being abused by her stepfather and Ice seems to have a soft spot for my COLLEGE aged part-time employee."

"She's twenty-one," he whispered. Darby gave him a sharp look and Gunner shook his head as if to say, don't go there.

"Ice…being the rescuer he is wants her to live here at the barn…in a room next to his and," she said looking behind her at Hawk and Eagle, "down the hall from the hypersexual nymphomaniac twins because that would be infinitely better than living anywhere else."

"Then…once you start tearing apart my store, you want me to shut it down for however long it takes to find this mysterious box. Do I have that right? Did I miss anything?" she asked. The guys looked at one another nodding their heads.

"Sounds about right baby, but let me clarify," said Gunner.

"Please...by all means, clarify," she said pulling out a chair. In solidarity, Grace and Kat sat next to her staring at Tango, Whiskey and Ghost who were seated as well.

"Listen baby...whoever this man is, he wants something that was hidden in that store. Now, we're still working on what or who owned it before you, but until then, we have to try to stop this maniac. Those men could have hurt Amanda and damned sure would have hurt you or Calla if you'd been there alone. We won't let you lose the store baby...I won't let you."

"How can you promise that Gunner?" she said leaning forward with tears in her eyes. "My whole life is in that store. And how do we know Olivia isn't the one behind all of this?"

"We don't honey, but that's why we need time to figure this shit out without you or Calla being harmed."

"And Amanda...what is that all about?" she said looking at Ice.

"Listen Darby, I know you don't know me well, but I have nothing but positive intentions with Amanda. Her stepdad is hurting her and if she stays there any longer, he's going to do more than hurt her. She's been living most of the time in her car, did you know that?" Darby shook her head, biting her lip.

"I just want to offer her a safe place to stay. She can work here at Club Steel until the store opens again...even after if she needs more hours. I will personally guarantee that Thing One and Thing Two stay away from her."

"Hey," said Hawk, "we're right here you know...we have feelings. You guys act like we're walking disease factories." Everyone raised an eyebrow and Hawk shrugged.

"I didn't mean to imply that," said Darby. "But I saw you guys go to your rooms last night with four girls...four!"

"Oh...we...we didn't take them inside the barn Darby. We'd never do that. We promise to stay away from Amanda. Besides, it looks like Ice has claimed her." Ice cursed under his breath, running his hands through his hair.

"I haven't claimed shit! I'm trying to help her that's all!"

"Oh, then I'm free to ask her out," said Eagle.

"Stay the fuck away from her," growled Ice.

"And there it is...he claimed her." Eagle said grinning. Ice could only shake his head looking back at Darby.

"Darby, I promise you I will take care of Amanda, you just let the guys worry about the store and this mysterious box."

"Okay." She stood from her seat, Kat taking one hand and Grace the other in solidarity. "You can close the store and do your thing, but if you hurt Amanda...if you destroy my store...I am going to be one pissed off mama." The three women turned and left the room as the men collectively let out a breath.

"Damn brother...she's kinda hot when she's pissed," said Razor.

"Shut the fuck up," he grinned nudging his brother. "We need to find this box and figure out what in the hell is in there and find out what connection, if any, Olivia Runyon has to all this."

"I think I can help with part of this," said Ace walking toward the group of men. "Darby's store was once a shipping store...you know like a mail place, not a post office, but sort of. There were P.O. boxes, shipping using a variety of vendors, packaging materials, that kind of shit."

"Damn, I don't remember that all," said Gunner.

"The dude that owned it, Jonah Haslett, died about a year ago. He had no family, nothing. The store was tied up in probate until the estate was settled. The realtor that Darby bought the building from, bought the building at auction hoping to flip it and make some cash."

"So, this Jonah Haslett had a box or something in that store that belonged to whoever Ascencio is working for?" asked Tango.

"I think so."

"And Olivia?" asked Gunner.

"Still working on that one brother. I sent Skull up to watch her for a few days. He's still there, but says she's going about her business as a wealthy Memphis socialite. She's going to be heading some charity event on Wednesday night. Skull got tickets and he's attending...tuxedo and all," grinned Ace.

"No shit," smiled Gunner, "I owe the brother a bottle of whiskey."

"Well, until then let's see if we can find that package," said Ghost. "Ice? Get the girl settled and show her the routine behind the bar, it will give the twins a break from bartender duty. Hawk? Eagle? Stay away from the girl."

"We got it," smiled Eagle. Ice eyed the two men, letting them know he wasn't going to tolerate their shit. They were both six-two and a solid two-hundred, but he wasn't exactly a small fry at six-one and two-o-five.

"Good, let's get this shit done so Calla can help my son learn to walk," smiled Ghost shaking his head. "Damn kid is somethin'."

CHAPTER TWENTY-TWO

Gunner went in search of Darby to make sure she was okay with their plan. He found her sitting on his back porch overlooking the valley, her knees pulled up to her chest, rocking back and forth in the swing. He stood at the door for a minute, just watching her. Her hair was like black satin sheets, shiny and straight to her shoulders. She was wearing another cute pair of shorts and the same t-shirt she'd put on that morning.

As he promised, he took the girls on a long drive and picnic, but of course their day ended abruptly with the issues at the book store. Calla was 'babysitting' with Grace and JT, while he sought out his love.

His love, he thought. Two weeks ago, he was a happily...well, semi-happy single man with no clue what was about to slam him in the face. He thought about calling his folks and took out his phone.

"Hey mom, how are you?"

"Gunner! Oh, honey we're all good here. Dad is out working on that old Ford of his...his happy place you know."

"Yea," he laughed, "I get it. How are Striker and Hunter?"

"They're both good, baby. Striker and Laura are buying a house down near the Keys. He just bought another vessel for the business." Gunner smiled at that. His brother never mentioned a love for deep sea fishing until he met Laura. Now, he was apparently going to own a fleet of deep-sea fishing boats. His father-in-law's idea of perfection, was simply a day on the boat catching the big one. Bored the shit out of Gunner, but he loved his brother for trying to make his wife happy.

"And Hunter?" he asked.

"Hunter's good...you know him...still not sure what he wants to be when he grows up, but he's doing good. He's working the lines in Alaska still. Makes great money, but damn I wish he'd settle down."

"He's still young mom. I'm forty so that makes Hunter...what...thirty-five?" he asked.

"I know how old my children are Gunner, I birthed them all. Now what about you, how are you?"

"Well, that's kind of why I'm calling mom. I've met someone...the one." He heard his mother gasp and could almost see her smiling.

"Oh Gunner...tell me all about her honey."

"She's amazing mom. She's so damned beautiful...all this jet-black hair and these huge almond eyes. She smells like...like rain and sunshine combined. Plus, she's super smart. She owns a bookstore downtown and she's got the cutest little girl on the planet mom."

"She's a mom," his mother sighed. "Oh Gunner...I knew your time was coming baby. How old is the little girl?"

"She's four going on twenty-four," he laughed. "Her name is Calla."

"Calla...like calla lily?" she asked.

"Yep...same thing I said to her when she told me her name. Told her that it was my moms' favorite flower so it must mean something. Darby...that's my girl...she's the best mom on the planet mom, and she's...well...you might not want to hear this, but she's just so fucking sexy mom. She's the only woman in the room...you know what I mean?"

"I know what you mean Gunner," she said laughing. "Your father still looks at me like I'm the only woman in the room and he treats me that way too. Oh, we can't wait to meet them."

"That's why I was calling, I was wondering if you and dad might want to come up. I'm trying to convince Darby to marry me and...well...if you were here..."

"Ammunition?" Gunner laughed nodding into the phone. "Listen Gunner, we'll come up there but don't you rush this girl into anything. She has that sweet little one to think of and you need to remember that. Everything in its' own time honey."

"I know mom. Talk to dad, I'd sure like you guys here soon...and Hunter and Striker too."

"I'll talk to all of them baby. You give that girl and her little one a kiss from us. Tell her she better get ready for some grandma love...oh hell...I'm gonna be a grandma! Ranger! We're gonna be grandparents! Gotta run honey, we'll call you in a few days."

Gunner laughed as he ended the call. He knew his parents would be thrilled with him finding the 'one'. Darby was still rocking on the back porch as he stepped outside.

"Hi baby," he said bending down to kiss her.

"Hi," she said quietly.

"You okay honey?" She nodded and then shook her head.

"I'm scared Gunner...what if...what if I lose the bookstore? What if something happens to Amanda...or worse...Calla..." He sat next to her on the swing and pulled her close.

"Darby? Do you trust me beautiful?" he asked quietly rocking with her.

"More than anyone in my entire life."

"Then trust me in this, you will not lose the bookstore, Amanda will be safe, and you and Calla will damn sure be safe. We are family honey...you, me and that little girl are family and I damned sure hope to make it permanent soon."

"Okay," she whispered, wiping her nose on the back of her hand.

"Okay? Okay as in okay you believe me, we're safe or okay as in you'll be my wife?" She smiled up at him, standing. She stepped back and shoved her shorts down, then pulled her t-shirt over her head.

"Okay make me your wife Gunner before you get me pregnant and I'm too fat to love," she smiled.

"Let me get this straight first," he said slapping her ass. She let out a loud yelp and blushed. "That's for believing that you pregnant would mean you're fat. This body full of my babies would be hot as fuck...don't ever doubt me in that again. And the getting married? Good thing you said yes, because I just invited my entire family up here in the next week or two."

"Gunner!"

"Shut up woman and make love to me."

CHAPTER TWENTY-THREE

Ice looked at the two suitcases in the trunk of Amanda's old two-door Volkswagen. The car had definitely seen better days and he wondered if there was even air conditioning or heat in the old junker. In the backseat was a pillow and blanket, shoes scattered on the floor. She really had been living out of her car and that pissed him off.

"Is this everything?" he asked.

"Yea," she said looking embarrassed. "I mean...I have a few things at the trailer, but it's nothing important."

"If it's yours Amanda, we'll go get it...together."

"You would do that?" she asked.

"You're damned right I would. Let's get your stuff up to your room, I'll show you around and then we can get whatever else belongs to you." She nodded, following him inside Club Steel. Opening the door, she was greeted by loud voices and the smells of something wonderful. Amanda stopped and stared at the men, who were very obviously staring back at her.

"It's okay, they're my friends and they know everything," he said.

"Everything Decker? Seriously?" He smiled looking down at her.

"It's what we do Amanda...we protect people and help them. They needed to know what was happening. Come on, let me introduce you." He set the suitcases down and then walked toward the table. "Everybody, this is Amanda our new bartender."

"Hey Amanda," came the chorus of voices.

"Amanda? This is Zulu, his wife Gabi...Whiskey and his wife Kat, Doc and his wife Bree, Tango, Razor, Ace, Axe, and...oh...that's Hawk and Eagle."

"I'll never be able to remember that," she said softly.

"No worries beautiful," said Tango, "there's no test. You just get yourself settled and then we can worry about training you on the bar."

"Yea...we'll do that in a bit," said Ice. "I'm going to take Amanda to her stepfather's place and pick up the rest of her things. Anyone want to ride along for fun?"

"Me!" yelled Tango.

"Me too!" said Razor jumping up and down excitedly. He looked down at her forearms seeing the bruises and cursed under his breath. "He do that to you?"

"Oh," said Amanda shoving her sleeves down, "it's no big deal...I mean...he doesn't like me much that's all."

"I don't care if he thinks you're the spawn of Satan darlin', no man puts his hands on a woman like that and leaves those kinds of marks. That's not a man, that's a spineless piece of shit." Razor smiled at her and she nodded.

"Th-thank you...all of you for saying that and for helping me. I'm sure I'll see you all in a few minutes." Amanda walked back toward her bags and Ice looked at Tango and Razor.

"Gives me great joy to know I'm going to beat the shit out of her stepfather," said Tango.

"Me too brother," said Razor. Ice shook his head smiling and followed Amanda. Taking her through the two steel doors, he explained the security and that she wasn't to let anyone past the doors...ever. She nodded, suddenly feeling safer than she had in her entire life. Walking up the stairs to the second floor they turned down a long hallway.

"My room is here," he said nodding to a doorway. He walked a few more feet. "This is yours." He opened the door and Amanda just stood in the doorway. There was a large overstuffed loveseat facing a big flat screen television on the wall. Behind it was a king-sized bed covered in a soft blue and white comforter, a side table with a lamp was on one side a small chair on the other.

Further in the room she noted the private bathroom with a huge farm sink and counter, the walk-in shower better than anything she'd ever seen in her life. He opened another door to a large closet, pointing to the built-in dresser. She nodded, then slid down the wall to the floor, sobbing.

"Amanda? Honey what's wrong? Tell me what do baby...do you need water? Food?" he asked kneeling in front of her. She shook her head.

"No...no...it's just...I've never had anything so nice in all my life. I can't believe I get to live here," she cried. Ice chuckled, pulling her against his shoulder, just rubbing her back.

"You're safe here," he said. "Let's get you up and get the rest of your things, okay? You can unpack when we get back and then we'll have dinner with the team." She nodded.

"Decker?" He turned to look at her as she walked toward him. Leaning up on her toes, she placed a soft kiss on his cheek. "Thank you." Ice watched as she walked out of the room and down the stairs. He couldn't move...he couldn't breathe.

Damn.

CHAPTER TWENTY-FOUR

Amanda wasn't kidding when she said she lived in a trailer park...and not the kind you see in Florida where people retire and have gardens, and big awnings. No, this shit was barely livable. There were rusted out cars parked in front of almost every trailer, kids' toys strewn across what little grass they had, and laundry hanging out on a line. Ice wondered if there was even running water in some of these places.

"It's pretty bad, isn't it?" she asked the car full of men, her face flush with embarrassment and shame.

"I've seen worse honey," said Tango, "but then again I was in the middle of a war zone in a foreign country...soooo..." She laughed and nodded.

"I know...believe me I know. It's why I don't have many friends. I never wanted to let anyone see this...didn't want to invite anyone home. My mom has been a drunk for as long as I can remember and my stepfather has been around since I was seven."

"What's his name Amanda?" asked Ice.

"Reginald." Ice nodded as they pulled in front of the beat-up trailer. The sun was blasting down and he noticed that several of the windows had no screens, but were wide open as well as the door. No air conditioning in this heat had to be fucking miserable. On a lounge chair sprawled out on the front lawn, was an older woman sound asleep, her dress askew, riding up her thighs.

"Oh God," whispered Amanda staring at her mothers' drunken form laid out for all to see. "I'm sorry you guys...that's my mother."

"We don't get to choose our parents Amanda," said Tango walking alongside her. She stopped next to the woman.

"Mom...mom!" she said louder, nudging the woman. She groaned and rolled to her side, her ass showing the underpants riding up her crack. "Shit...Mom!"

"Hmmm...oh its' my baby girl...Manda Panda...Manda," she slurred.

"Mom, I'm getting my things and then I'm leaving...I won't be coming back here mom."

"Yea...yea that's good. Reginal' was lookin' for you baby...you need to do as he says...give him what he wants." Ice wanted to tear the woman apart, but he knew in her drunken state she wouldn't remember anything...if ever. Amanda walked up the rickety wooden steps and through the door, her eyes adjusting to the light. Before she could even get two feet inside, big hands gripped her shoulders, shoving her against the wall, the smell of alcohol and body odor assaulting her senses.

"There's the fucking slut," he growled, "time to pay your rent bitch." He started to unbuckle his jeans when he felt big hands at his neck squeezing. Amanda watched as his face turned purple, Tango helping her up off the floor.

"You okay honey?" he asked. She nodded, swallowing the sob threatening to escape. "Go get what's yours. We'll handle this." She turned moving to the back bedroom and they could hear her shuffling around.

"Who the fuck do you think you are coming in my home?" Reginald was probably five-foot-eight, but he was easily two-hundred and fifty pounds. His mass would have overtaken Amanda eventually and there was no doubt to anyone standing there, what his intentions were.

"I'm the man that's going to kick your ass you fat prick," said Ice with snarl. "You touched that girl…your stepdaughter."

"Didn't fuck her yet if that's what you're worried about," he grinned. Ice slammed his fist into his gut and the man gasped for air doubling over. "What was that for? Girl owes me rent...fucking cunt won't put out she owes me..." Slam! A fist to the face.

"Slow learner isn't he brother?" said Razor grinning at the disgusting man in front of him.

"You won't fucking touch her ever again. She's leaving here today and will never return," Ice said pulling out the long thin blade he always carried with him. "If I ever see you come near her, if you even walk down the same street as her...I will gut you like the pig you are. I will cut that teeny tiny dick of yours off and feed it to you piece by piece."

"Was that clear to you Reggie?" asked Tango.

"She aint' nothin' special...thinks she is...holdin' out...being stingy with that pussy..." SLAM!

"He really is dumb as shit," growled Razor. "Listen old man...simple as this...come near her...die." Razor let his foot fly straight into the man's groin and he sucked in a breath, trying and failing to get air into his lungs.

"Clear now?" asked Ice. The man nodded, not able to say a word. Amanda walked out of the back room, looking down at her stepfather. He snarled at her, but she ignored him, stepping over his fat legs.

"Don't you try to come back bitch!" he yelled. Tango took her two large duffel bags and she turned toward the old man. Doubling her fist, she slammed it straight into his nose.

"That felt wonderful!" she said shaking out her hand. "On second thought, that hurt like hell." Ice laughed kissing her forehead.

"Let's get some ice on that honey. Come on, let's go home." Amanda nodded walking out the door and taking one last look at her mothers' sleeping form. She would remember nothing tomorrow, maybe not even remember that she had a daughter. Today, she was going home. Home. She'd never have to return here again. Home.

By the time Amanda unpacked and made it back downstairs, the team was all seated with a full house in Club Steel, ordering dinner and just having a normal conversation without drunkenness and without violence. Amanda thought it was the most amazing thing ever. She smiled at Darby, her friend and boss.

Sunday night was always busy, but in the summer months they offered karaoke on Sunday night. Amanda smiled at the man trying to sing a George Strait song, but failing miserably. Sitting next to Ice, wincing at the sour note, she turned and smiled at him.

"I guess he gets an "A" for effort, right?" she said smiling.

"It's kind of a tradition around here...or at least a new tradition," said Grace. "We started doing it back in May and the crowds loved it. Everyone has to sing for their supper." Amanda looked at the woman and stood, leaving the table. A few minutes later she returned with a violin in her hands, waiting her turn at the microphone.

"What the hell?" said Ice watching her climb on the small dais set up as a stage. Amanda stepped up to the microphone and cleared her throat, blushing.

"This is for my supper...and...and my new friends," she said smiling. She raised the bow and caressed the strings, the sweet melody of a familiar song floating through the restaurant. Where there was once noise and chatter, there was now complete silence and awe as she played and began to sing. The haunting melody floating over the crowd, the tones nothing short of perfection, each note played or sung with passion.

When the rain
Is blowing in your face
And the whole world
Is on your case
I could offer you
A warm embrace
To make you feel my love

When the evening shadows
And the stars appear
And there is no one there
To dry your tears
I could hold you
For a million years
To make you feel my love

I know you
Haven't made
Your mind up yet
But I would never
Do you wrong
I've known it
From the moment
That we met
No doubt in my mind
Where you belong

I'd go hungry
I'd go black and blue
I'd go crawling
Down the avenue
No, there's nothing
That I wouldn't do
To make you feel my love

The storms are raging
On the rolling sea
And on the highway of regret
Though winds of change
Are throwing wild and free
You ain't seen nothing
Like me yet

I could make you happy
Make your dreams come true
Nothing that I wouldn't do
Go to the ends
Of the Earth for you
To make you feel my love
To make you feel my love

Amanda let the violin slip from her chin, holding the bow against its' neck. She looked at the shocked faces and then heard the thunderous applause. Smiling, she stepped down off the dais and walked to the table.

"Did I earn my supper?" she asked smiling as Ice stood and hugged her gently to his chest. He leaned close to her ear and whispered.

"You're the most beautiful thing ever." Amanda felt herself blush and then looked at Ghost.

"You earned your supper, lunch, breakfast and snacks for a year!" said Ghost. "That was fucking amazing kid."

"Amanda," said Darby, "I'm assuming that you're a music major." The girl nodded shyly. "Why didn't you tell me you were a music major...why would you keep that from me?"

"I don't know. I guess it didn't matter...I mean you own a book store, not a music store. I'm not even sure what kind of job I'm going to get," she said shyly. "I actually like teaching the violin and guitar...I can play both, but private lessons don't make me enough money to live off. I have to say, I was shocked when I went back and my violin wasn't broken. Reginald broke two others and they weren't cheap. I can't thank you enough for helping me get this one."

"Amanda you should be singing professionally," said Ice. "That was the most beautiful thing I've ever heard."

"It really was honey," said Darby hugging her.

"Thank you, but I'm not a fan of singing in front of huge crowds. I've tried, believe me. I prefer things like this where it's small intimate gatherings...maybe I could sing once in a while?" she said looking at Ghost.

"You want to sing? Here? In this bar?" She nodded grinning at him.

"I wouldn't charge you or anything...I just like doing it. Maybe...maybe one night a week or something...just for tips."

"Fucking done," said Ghost grinning at the young girl.

"Really?" she asked excitedly. "Oh my God, I can't believe this! You have no idea how much that will help me!"

"Believe it beautiful," said George. "That was some of the finest singin' I've ever heard and you're playin'...honey that was like music from the angels themselves."

By the time the meal was done, the team encouraged Amanda to sing another song. This time she chose a beautiful Irish reel, with very little vocals but a hauntingly gorgeous violin piece. The couples danced slowly, taking in the music and all Ice could thing was he wished he were dancing with her to this music. As they finished, each slowly made their way to bed, all exhausted. There was a lot to do at the bookstore and still a box to find.

Outside her room, Ice stopped and shoved his hands in his pockets smiling down at her.

"You shocked the shit out of me Amanda. That was fucking incredible honey," he said smiling down at her.

"Thank you…not just for that, but for everything today Decker. I'll see you tomorrow?" she asked. He nodded like a schoolboy and she stepped forward. Standing on her toes once again, this time she placed a soft kiss on his lips and flushed a bright pink. "Good night Decker."

"Good night beautiful." He waited until he heard her lock engage and then went into his room, falling on his back against the bed. *Great…blue balls for me.*

CHAPTER TWENTY-FIVE

Darby stepped from the shower pulling on her pajama shorts and tank top, then walked down the hall to check on Calla. She wanted to go back to the apartment, but Gunner convinced her it wasn't safe until they could figure out what this damned box was all about. She heard soft murmurs as she approached her daughters' room and smiled. She should have known that Gunner would get her tucked into bed.

"So, the beast told the girl if she stayed with him, he would let her father go free, but she had to stay with him forever," said Gunner.

"Did she stay?" asked Calla filled with curiosity and a little fear.

"She did, because she loved her father so much. She wanted him to have his freedom, but she also saw something in the beast...something others didn't. The girl knew that he wasn't just a beast, he was a real person under there and maybe if she were kind to him, he would be kind to her."

"So maybe...if I'm nice to Jacob, he might be nice to me?" asked Calla innocently. Gunner kissed the top of her head and smiled. The little shit Jacob was probably just an asshole, but he wouldn't tell this sweet little thing that. Calla would discover in her own time that boys were often mean to girls when they liked them, but until then, he would protect her as best he could.

"Maybe, but if he's mean to you Calla, you don't have to take it. Tell an adult first, but if he keeps saying and doing mean things to you, tell your mommy or me...okay?"

"Okay Gunner and you'll protect me?"

"Always beautiful."

"Gunner? I know you and mommy aren't married yet but...can I call you daddy yet?" she asked looking up to him.

"I..."

"Yes," said Darby walking into the room. Gunner looked up with shock on his face. "Yes, you can honey, if Gunner says it's okay. Gunner and mommy are getting married and he'll be your daddy soon...so yes, you can call Gunner daddy now if...if he's okay with that." Gunner's eyes filled with tears and he swallowed, trying to control his emotions.

"It's more than okay with me," he whispered against Calla's soft hair.

"Goodnight daddy," she said snuggling down in the covers.

"Goodnight sweet girl," he said kissing her head. Darby kissed her daughters head and turned off the light, then taking Gunner's hand, led him back downstairs to the living room. Gunner pulled her next to him as they sprawled out on the sofa, the television on, but not really a focus for them.

"Thank you, Darby, thank you baby," he said with a tear in his eye.

"Gunner, you've done nothing but show me exactly the kind of man you are...loving, loyal, fiercely protective. You are going to be a great father to Calla and I know you're going to be the man I've dreamed of as my husband. I'm still scared...scared that I'll wake up and this will all be a dream, but until then, I'm going to embrace it...and you."

"My beautiful girl...I'm so in love with you Darby. Calla was like having the icing on my cake. You were both such a surprise in my life I didn't think it would ever happen. As a Marine, I've seen a lot...maybe too much. Part of why Ghost and our team left the service was something horrific that happened to a bunch of little girls. We did what was right and we'll stand by that until the day we all die, but I knew then that if I ever had the privilege of becoming a father, I would protect my child and my wife with everything I have in me."

"I never doubted that for a moment Gunner," she said smiling.

"So...I heard you say you're going to marry me soon," he said grinning against her hair, "when should I tell my folks to get up here?" Darby chuckled against his chest, settling her chin against her folded hands, looking up at him.

"Why don't we try for the fourth of July weekend? I mean, it falls on a Friday...we could get married on the Saturday and it's only two weeks away. That would give me time to get everything settled."

"I think that's perfect baby, I'll text mom and dad now," he said grabbing his phone and typing out the text. They were most likely already asleep but he would wake to a series of screaming texts from his family, and that made him smile.

"Gunner? If we do this..."

"When we do this," he countered.

"When," she smiled, "it might trigger something that lets Olivia know where I am. I mean, it looks like she doesn't have anything to do with what's happening with the store, but I still worry that she might try to get to Calla."

"Let me worry about that beautiful." She nodded, kissing his jaw. Darby pushed his t-shirt up over his head and then worked her way down his chest, placing her warm lips on his flesh as she crawled down his body. His big hands gripped her hair, holding her still for a moment, but when she looked up grinning, he was lost.

Darby tasted his skin, the taste of his soap and a musky manliness that made her wet and warm. She pushed his pajama pants down his hips, the deep vee of his muscles so sexy, she let her tongue trail along both sides. Gripping his cock in her tiny hand, he moaned as her tongue flicked out to lick that sweet, salty taste of his precum.

She opened her mouth, taking in the thick purple head, her tongue wrapping around it and then licking down as she gripped his balls.

"Fuck baby..." he moaned. She let a low hum escape her lips as she continued to work him, her jaw opening wider to take him deep. Gunner thrust his hips forward on instinct and she sucked him in, feeling his big cock hit the back of her throat, she opened wider.

Darby's hands gently massaged his full, tight balls, her fingers gliding behind the heavy sacs along the thin line that sent him overboard.

"Jesus...Darby..." he groaned. She nodded and continued to suck and finger his delicate flesh. As his hips moved faster toward her mouth, she sucked harder until he gripped her head, holding her in place. She felt the hot spurt of liquid in her mouth and swallowed, the taste of him salty and warm. He filled her mouth and she just continued to swallow until the last drop was licked clean from his beautiful thick cock.

Darby looked up at him smiling, placing a small kiss at the tip of his dick.

"Fucking hell woman...that was...that was..."

"Good?"

"Good? It was fucking great baby...come here...let me return the favor," he said pulling her toward him. Darby shook her head, blushing.

"I...I'm on my period...I started this afternoon," she said blushing.

"Sweet girl, if you think that's going to keep me from touching you, you're wrong," he said pulling her closer.

"Gunner you can't!"

"Can and will," he said tearing of her clothes. "Let me do this baby...you'll see." Gunner pulled one of her nipples between his teeth and sucked as she let out a long gasp. He squeezed the other breast, pinching her nipple as he did and he felt them get hard and erect. Lying her flat on the sofa, he took turns with each beautiful breast as her body writhed beneath his hands. Sliding his fingers over her hard little nub, he rubbed back and forth.

"Oh...oh damn...Gunner..." she moaned. He grinned at her as he took her nipple between his teeth and pulled, roughly squeezing her clit, then rubbing it vigorously until she shook with satisfaction. Gunner smiled down at her.

"Open your eyes baby," he said kissing her lips. "Open Darby...nothing to be embarrassed about honey."

"Jesus Gunner...I've never...I mean, I didn't know a man would do that...while I was..."

"What? That a man would want to have crazy, sexy fucking orgasms with you while you were on your period?" She nodded blushing. "Darby baby, your body is gorgeous all the time. If I didn't touch you for the five or six days you were bleeding that would only leave me with a lousy twenty-four days a month to love on you. That's just not good enough for me. Unless a doctor tells me, I can't touch you...that I'll hurt you…you can be damned sure I'm going to be touching, loving, fucking this body every damned day. Clear?"

"Clear," she said smiling up at him. "Now…let me enjoy this beautiful…[lick]…thick…[lick]…cock…[lick] again. Because I am learning that my man loves to be sucked almost as much as he loves to be fucked."

"Damn woman…you are going to make me happy for the next sixty years."

"That's the plan handsome…that's the plan."

CHAPTER TWENTY-SIX

As he'd predicated, Gunner woke to twenty-six text messages from his mother, father, and brothers, all congratulating him and ensuring him they would be there by the Wednesday before the wedding. He smiled reading the messages from his brothers.

The great Gunner has fallen…alert the presses!

Seriously bro…congratulations!

Awesome…a niece and a sister-in-law right away…fucking over-achiever

At breakfast, he and Darby spoke to Calla about the wedding and she was so excited, she could hardly be contained. Darby was taking the next few days off until they could find the damned box, but once that was done, she would be moving their things into Gunners'...their house.

"Will my new aunt and uncles and grandma and grandpa like me?" asked Calla.

"Are you kidding me?" said Gunner. "They're gonna love you! My brothers are going to make it a competition for who can be your favorite uncle."

"Wow...I have a lot of uncles," she said smiling. "Will...will my grandma make me follow lots of rules?"

"No baby," said Gunner. "The only rule this grandma will have is you have to give lots of kisses and you have to wash your hands. That will be the extent of her control."

"Go get your backpack baby," said Darby. The little girl bounced away up the stairs and Gunner looked at Darby. "What?"

"Does she have to go to school? I mean...I'd love to keep her close until we figure all this mess out honey."

"I know you want to keep her close, but the school is right down the street from the store Gunner. You can drop her off and pick her up. She'll be fine." He nodded, still not convinced but he knew she was right. The entire team would literally be two blocks away if anything happened. He would just have to warn the daycare provider to be extra cautious with any unexpected visitors.

Calla came down the stairs in her little dress, her Dora backpack and a huge smile.

"Can we take the motorcycle?" she asked.

"Not today baby," he said smiling at her. "Besides, I need to get you a helmet and a leather jacket. You can't ride on the motorcycle without that...safety first, okay?" She let her lip stick out for a half a second and then nodded, running out the front door toward the barn. Racing in the back door, she rushed into the kitchen to find who she was looking for.

"Uncle Tango! Can I ride your motorcycle without a helmet and leather jacket?" Gunner stood in the doorway with his arms crossed, Darby watching Tango mull over his reply.

"Uh...well...I don't think that's very safe, do you?" She looked at him with tears in her eyes and he almost caved. "Have you ever fallen on the sidewalk and skinned your knee really bad?"

"Yea...Jacob pushed me and it hurt really bad. It bleeded and I had a big scab and bandage," she said sniffing. That little shit Jacob again.

"Okay, well if you rode my motorcycle without a helmet or jacket, it would be like that only way worse!" he said waving his big arms around.

"Oh."

"Yea, oh...so why don't we wait until you're safe and then I promise I'll take you on a ride if your mommy and Gunner..."

"Daddy...I get to call him daddy now," she said flashing a huge smile almost as big as Gunner's. The entire room smiled at the little girl and then back to Gunner.

"Fu...fudging fantastic dude," said Tango grinning at his friend. "As I was saying if daddy says it's okay then I'll take you...deal?"

"Deal," she said nodding her head. "Uncle George can we make cupcakes for my Fourth of July play?"

"We sure can darlin'. I'll get all the stuff and we'll make them the day before."

"Red, white and blue Uncle George…you know that right?" she said looking at him with earnest.

"Are you sure?" he grinned. "I was thinking pink with sprinkles and maybe unicorns." Calla bit her lip thinking about it for a minute.

"Maybe for my birthday…red, white, and blue for my play." He nodded giving her the thumbs up. Gunner kissed Darby on the cheek and then looked at the team.

"Folks are coming up next week with my brothers. Darby and I are getting married next Saturday." The cheers were loud and Calla jumped up and down, cheering with them. She walked over to JT and kissed his soft cheek.

"You'll be my real cousin then JT," she whispered. Ghost smiled at the little girl, shaking his head. Gunner reached out for her.

"Come on sweet girl, let's get you to school." She jumped in his arms and they took off down the hallway, Tango, Razor, Eagle, Hawk, and Axe following. Gabi waddled through the door; her enormous belly barely concealed beneath the huge t-shirt belonging to her husband.

"Oh honey," said Darby watching the woman. "Come. Sit here."

"I need these babies to come now," she said looking at the group. "I'm serious you guys...I can't do this another four weeks."

"Let's go for a walk," said Kat smiling at the other women.

"Yea," said Grace. "A walk is good for you. Let's get you some fresh air and a little exercise, you'll feel better." Grace could see the look of relief on Zulu's face and smiled at him. The women rallied together taking Gabi out through the back porch. Ghost watched the women leave, still holding his son firmly in his arms.

"Brother if she doesn't give birth soon, I'm never getting sex again," groaned Zulu. Ghost smiled, nodding at his friend.

"I tell you what," said George turning around with a frustrated expression on his face, "why don't you carry not one, but two lives in your belly for forty weeks, gain thirty pounds of water and twenty pounds of other weight, let your ankles swell, your body bloat, your boobs get huge, your bladder get small, and your emotions ride on the worst seas of your life and let me know how worried you are about sex."

Zulu looked at the older man and back at Whiskey, Doc, and Ghost who were grinning at him.

"Damn George, that's an awful lot of knowledge for a man who doesn't have children," said Zulu.

"I got all of you! Like a bunch of damn children. I listen to them girls. I heard when Gracie was puking her guts up, pregnant and bloated and feeling unattractive. I heard when poor Gabi was feeling her body get bigger by the day. I listen. 'Bout damn time you boys did the same."

Zulu looked at Ghost, then back at Whiskey and Doc.

"If you idiots would pay attention, you'd see what's right in front of you. You'd see the subtle changes in their bodies, in their behavior. 'Sposed to be elite warriors...pfft! Elite my ass...miss what's right in front of 'ya." He said stirring the pot of sauce for tonight's special.

"What are you talking about George?" asked Whiskey eyeing the old man carefully.

"I'm talking about you openin' yer damned eyes! See that yer girl is bigger up top than she was a few weeks ago. And you...'sposed to be a nurse or some damned thing...how about you notice that Bree has been moody and crying at the drop of a hat. I swear to God ya'll are dumb as shit. Both them girls are pregnant and don't even know yet."

"Wh-what?" said Doc sitting there wide-eyed.

"I...but Kat..." Whiskey stammered. Ghost just grinned at both the men, then winked at George.

"Maybe you boys should go pick up a few pregnancy tests," said Ghost. George moved around the counter, reaching inside the pantry he pulled out a big box.

"No need. I bought two dozen a few weeks ago. Take two and go find yer damned women."

CHAPTER TWENTY-SEVEN

Gunner happily carried Calla into school, her arms possessively wound around his neck. He reluctantly set her down, kissing her soft cheek, telling her to join the other children. Tango stood behind him watching the scene, grinning at his friend. He'd known Gunner for almost twenty-five years and never saw him like he'd been these past few weeks. The receptionist looked up at Tango and gave a lazy smile.

"Morning," he said politely.

"Are you Calla's dad?" she asked. Tango shook his head.

"Nope...that would be Gunner. I'm her uncle. Hey? Where is the kid named Jacob?" he asked. The woman looked around the big open space and pointed to a boy by the swings with a light blue shirt on. He was bigger than the other kids and Tango saw that attitude right away. He was a bully.

Walking toward the kid, he stopped in front of him looking down, ensuring that his size made the little boy a tad frightened.

"You Jacob?" he asked. The little boy nodded. "I'm Calla's uncle and that's her dad. You should be nicer to her."

"I don't hafta be nice," he said sticking out his chin defiantly.

"Everyone has to be nice kid...everyone." Jacob looked down at his shoes and something about that made Tango think the boy was mimicking what he saw at home. He knelt in front of the boy. "Listen kid. Nobody likes a bully...nobody. It's okay to stick up for yourself or even to stick up for kids who are smaller than you. You're a big boy and the little ones look up to you. Don't screw it up, okay?" He nodded, swallowing the tears threatening to spill and Tango stood, leaving him there.

"Just couldn't help yourself, could you?" grinned Gunner.

"Man...something about that kid tells me he's seeing that at home." Tango and Gunner started to head toward the front door when the receptionist stopped him.

"That was really nice of you. I tell Joan all the time that she needs to have a chat with him, but she says her husband is in charge of the discipline with Jacob." Realization hit Gunner and he knew exactly what was happening. He shot a text to Bree to remind her about having a conversation with Joan at the gym if she saw her.

"Let's go man," said Tango. Walking back toward the bookstore he stopped at the coffee shop to grab some pastries and coffee for the team...or at least that's what he told himself. "Hey Taylor."

"Oh...hi Tango. What can I get for you today?" she said blushing.

"Five coffees and a dozen pastries...just whatever you have," he said grinning at her. He watched her pour the coffees, then carefully place the pastries in the box. Gunner nudged him and he shook his head.

"Brother," he whispered, "she's beautiful. Just ask her out." Tango let out a long breath and looked up to see Taylor staring at him, her hands holding the tray of coffee and box of pastries. Gunner reached for them and turned to leave them alone.

"So, Taylor...I was wondering...we're having a big Fourth of July celebration out at the barn. Would you like to..."

"Yes!" she said excitedly and then blushed. Tango laughed and nodded at her. "Sorry. Yes. I've been hoping you'd ask me out."

"Wish you woulda told me honey," he grinned. "I was thinking I'm too old for you."

"Too old? Tango just how old do you think I am?" she asked.

"I don't know...mid-twenties?"

"You're sweet Tango, but I'm thirty-four." His eyes went wide and his smile even wider. "Can I ask your real name?

"Tyler."

"Tyler," she repeated extending her hand, "it's nice to meet you, Tyler. I'm Taylor and I look forward to spending the Fourth with you." Tango was lost for words. He stood there just holding her hand when the guy behind him nudged him.

"Buddy you gonna let go of her hand so I can get my damned coffee?" Tango turned, giving the man a look of death and then turned back to Taylor giving her a wink.

"I'll be back at lunch...to eat I mean...and to see you," he said walking out the door. Taylor graced him with a huge smile helping the man waiting for his coffee. By the time he got to the bookstore the guys were all looking at him with shit-eating grins and lovesick eyes.

"Fuck off!" he yelled, inwardly smiling. "Let's get to work."

Carefully, methodically, the men searched the bottom floor, tapping on walls searching for hollow spaces or secret compartments. It was a painstaking process mapping out squares of the walls to test and then moving onto the next. At lunch, Taylor brought over sandwiches for the guys, although they all knew it was really for Tango.

By mid-afternoon they were beyond frustrated.

"Do we take out the floors tomorrow?" asked Tango. Gunner shook his head.

"I don't know man. We start doing that, we're going to be moving shelving, books, everything. I just don't think that's something we want to tackle." The bell above the door rang and Taylor walked back in with cookies and more coffee.

"I thought you guys might need this," she said with a smile.

"Thank you," said Tango.

"Darby said you guys were looking for something that the previous owner might have left. Mr. Haslett was a quirky old man," she said looking around the room.

"You knew him?" asked Tango. She nodded, smiling at him.

"Yea. I mean, I spent every summer here as a kid with my grandparents. I'd run over here if they had something to ship or something that came in. Bought stamps from him, that sort of thing. I never understood how he could stay in business. I mean this is a small town with small town values. The Post Office is like the extension of a town hall or church here."

"But he was busy?" asked Eagle.

"Yea...I mean there wasn't a lot of foot traffic, but he had more drop offs and deliveries than I could keep track of. He had really weird hours too. My grandparents always opened at six...I open at seven now, but they were early risers. We closed at four. But he would sometimes be open at four or five in the morning and close the rest of the day, then open back up at eight or nine. It was just...quirky."

"Did you ever see anyone strange going in and out? Maybe the same person all the time, but no one you knew?" She shook her head.

"I don't think so, but remember I was just a teenager, then a college kid when I was here. I probably didn't notice much back then. He was always nice to me, but...I don't know...almost guarded. I asked him if he needed extra help when I was in college. I was looking for more hours and thought I could work some evening shifts for him. He practically took my head off. Said he always closed at five, but I knew that wasn't true. Like I said...odd...eccentric maybe."

"Was he married? Kids?" She shook her head again.

"So, you're looking for something he left behind?"

"Yea, we just don't really know what it is," said Gunner frustrated.

"Well, Mr. Haslett was terrible about the upkeep of this place. My grandparents were always on him since we shared the south wall. Their big beef was that he never got the old plumbing repaired."

"What do you mean hun?" asked Tango.

"You didn't know?" They all shook their heads. "Oh…well my grandparents were here when it happened, but the pipes used to burst every winter. Mr. Haslett was too cheap to repair them all and my grandparents knew when the weather would get really cold, it was going to happen. They had our walls reinforced, but if you were looking for something of value from him, I'd suspect he put up, not down."

"Up?" asked Eagle.

"Yea…either in the apartment or in the attic," she smiled. "Well, gotta get back. See you tomorrow Tango." He nodded looking at the beautiful young woman walking out and then turned to the others.

"Fucking hell, we've been looking in the wrong place. Let's start at the top and work our way down," said Tango. Gunner nodded.

"Be back in ten, gotta pick up Calla," he said heading out the door. The others moved upstairs through the apartment and found the attic stairs, giving them a tug. Hawk crawled up first, finding a small string attached the lone light bulb.

"See anything?" asked Tango. He heard Hawk moving carefully along the rafter, his big body making the old wood creak and groan with every step. "Hawk don't make me climb up there and kick your damned ass." There was complete silence for a few long seconds and then just three simple words echoes throughout the room.

"Holy...fucking...shit."

CHAPTER TWENTY-EIGHT

Gunner walked back into the bookstore to see the team seated on the floors just chatting, eating cookies and drinking their coffee.

"Break time?" he asked raising an eyebrow as he set Calla down.

"You need to see something," said Hawk standing.

"Stay here baby," said Gunner. "Why don't you get a book and show uncle Eagle how good you read?" She nodded and skipped toward the children's' section. He could hear Eagle holler at her.

"Get the one about the monkey!"

Gunner followed Hawk up the steps to the apartment and then to the attic stairs letting him go up first and then he followed. At the top of the stairs, he let his eyes adjust to the light, or lack thereof, and then swallowed. Holy fuck!

"What do we do?" asked Hawk.

"Our guy said it was one box, right?" asked Gunner looking at the mess in the attic.

"Yep...one fucking box. Those...are all boxes...of dynamite. My guess is from thirty or forty years ago. This all used to be mining country, so maybe he kept it from those days, who in the hell knows. I'd be worried that shit is unstable as all fuck though." Gunner nodded.

"The other boxes, we didn't dig into yet. The bags? That's pretty easy to see brother…cocaine. Pure as shit cocaine. What the fuck was that old man doing?"

"I would bet he was shipping and receiving merchandise for someone or was the middle man at least. Right now, before we touch anything, we have to get that fucking dynamite out of here and not alert the whole damned town that an entire block could blow without warning," said Gunner.

"I think we should get Calla home and get the rest of the guys up here tonight," said Hawk. "Between my brother and I and Razor, we know enough about explosives to get this shit out of here safely. We'll make sure the blasting caps are removed. Depending on how old they are, the nitro might be deactivated, but I just don't know man. It's not like there's an expiration date on this shit."

"Fuck," he mumbled. "If this shit blows now, we not only have an explosion, but we have a shit ton of cocaine blowing in the air. The whole fucking town would be high." Hawk couldn't help but grin, nodding at the picture that created.

"Okay," said Gunner, "let's get Calla back home and explain this shit to Ghost. We'll get as many men as we can spare back here and remove the dynamite tonight. If we can get that done, then we can focus on what's in those boxes. Once I have the boxes opened and figure out what the fuck this dude is looking for, I'll call the DEA to pick up the coke."

"Let's go," said Hawk. "And Gunner...step lightly huh?"

Gunner let out a long slow breath and nodded, carefully taking the steps one at a time. They were both concerned about putting the steps back up, in case that movement set everything moving. Back downstairs, they all waited to see his reaction. Looking at Calla curled in Eagles' lap he controlled his language.

"Sugar bumps and fudge mounds," he spit out. The men all grinned at him and Calla laughed.

"I know you wanna say bad words," said Calla, "but if you do mommy will be really mad."

"I know princess, which is why daddy is trying really hard to not say the bad words." He looked at Eagle who had Calla wrapped in his arms protectively. "Did uncle Eagle read with you baby?"

"I had to read to him daddy, he was having trouble with some of the words," she said. Eagle shrugged his shoulders, but held the little girl closer, a wash of protectiveness flooding his body.

"Let's lock up...carefully and let Ghost know what's going on. Tango? You might want to ask Taylor to close up shop for the night. Tell her what you think she can tolerate." He nodded heading out the door to see the woman next door.

Gunner locked the front doors and waited for Tango to finish, seeing him speaking to Taylor through the big glass window. Eagle took Calla by the hand and entered the shop.

"Hi Taylor," said Calla excitedly. "Uncle Eagle says I can get a cupcake."

"He did huh? Well, that's a pretty nice uncle," she said smiling. She put the cupcake in a box and took Eagle's money. "You're sure a lucky girl to get a daddy and all these handsome uncles all at once."

"I'm the luckiest! And guess what? Jacob was nice to me today!" She skipped out the door with Eagle and Tango turned to Taylor.

"Suddenly nice to her, huh?" Tango shrugged.

"So anyway, I just need you to trust me honey. Close up early. Give me your number and I'll call to let you know when it's safe to come back."

"Tango, I can't just close up. This is my life. I'll lose too much revenue."

"Honey, I promise whatever revenue you lose we'll replace. Just trust me...please." She nodded agreeing to close an hour early and Tango figured it was a good victory. Enough for today anyway...enough for today.

CHAPTER TWENTY-NINE

The group of men and one small little girl walked in the doors looking defeated and exhausted. Darby stood and walked toward Gunner, recognizing the need for touch in that moment. She wrapped her arms around his waist, laying her head against his chest as he kissed her.

"Nothing?" she asked.

"Let's get everyone together honey...okay?" he said. She nodded but frowned. Taking Calla to the kitchen, she asked George if he would look after her while the grown-ups talked. George was more than happy to have the company of someone who actually listened to him. In the dining room, the entire team pulled tables' together, sitting, waiting for Gunner to tell them what they'd found.

"What's up brother?" asked Ghost sitting next to Grace, the baby monitor gripped firmly in her hand.

"Dynamite and cocaine...that's what is up," he said with a loud pop of the 'p'.

"Say again?" said Ghost with a surprised expression.

"Cases of dynamite, probably thirty or forty years old and at least a dozen blocks of cocaine. There are some boxes as well, like hard bodied luggage, but I didn't dare open them with the dynamite up there."

"Fuck," said Zulu swallowing, looking down at Gabi's big belly. "I've never had to work with dynamite. Eagle? Hawk? Razor?"

"Never," said Hawk. Eagle shook his head as well.

"I did," said Razor. "My uncle owned a turquoise mine in Mexico. We would go down there every summer and I would help him in the mines. They used dynamite all the time. Shit is totally unpredictable if it's old. We need to get the caps off and then carefully move that shit away."

"That's exactly what Hawk said." Gunner nodded at the younger man and he grinned. "I figured we'd go back up tonight, get the dynamite out of there and then tomorrow we can try to figure out what's in the boxes. Once we know what's in there, we can remove those and then call the DEA to pick up the drugs."

"Sounds like a plan," said Ghost. "Who do you need?"

"Don't wanna force anyone to go brother," said Gunner. "Obviously would love to have Eagle, Hawk, and Razor. Zulu? You need to stay put brother. Doc...Whiskey..."

"They just found out Kat and Bree are both pregnant," said Grace.

"Oh fuck!" said Gunner smiling. "Damn! Congratulations guys...seriously that's awesome!"

Whiskey smiled at his friend and pulled Kat tighter to his body, while Bree started to cry, something George noticed about her before anyone else.

"God, I'm such a mess," she said sniffling.

"You're not a mess baby...you're pregnant and hormonal, there's a difference. What you are is beautiful and carrying our child." Bree kissed her husband and the others' all grinned. There would be five babies all under a year by the time all was said and done. That was going to be some scary shit.

"Okay, so Hawk, Eagle, Razor, and..."

"Me," said Ice.

"And me," said Axe. Gunner nodded at both men giving them a silent thank you. Standing at the bar Amanda watched the interactions and said nothing when she heard Ice volunteer for whatever it was he was volunteering for. She carefully set the glasses on the bar and focused on her task at hand.

"Any clue what's in those boxes?" asked Ghost.

"None...we still don't even know who it is this guy works for. We know the two assholes we caught the other day were working for Javier Ascencio, but we don't know who Javier is working for or what he's looking for." Gunner was frustrated with the whole damned thing. Someone was screwing with their lives and threatening the lives of his woman and girl.

"Okay..."

"Ooooookay," said Gabi. Ghost looked at her and she grinned.

"Okay..."

"Ooooookay...okay...okay," she repeated. Ghost eyed the woman and then looked down, seeing the puddle beneath her feet. Zulu simply stared at his wife wondering why she was acting so strange.

"Oh damn," said Ghost pointing to the floor.

"Fuck!" yelled Zulu standing so quickly his chair went flying backwards. "A doctor...Doc...get a doctor...I mean get you...get..."

"Calm down brother," said Doc standing calmly. "Let's get her to the hospital..."

"NOOOOOOO...." screamed Gabi. "No...no time...now...coming now!"

"Shit!" said Doc racing toward her. "Zulu get her upstairs to the treatment room. Grace and Darby, you've both had babies, come with me." The women nodded running up the stairs to prep the table and make sure Doc had what he needed. Zulu carried his wife up the stairs with some difficulty, although he would never tell her that. He gently lay his wife on the table, while the others waited outside the door.

"Hey Doc...no offense, but could you look away when..."

"Don't fuck with me Quin!" said Gabi. "I'm about to spit out two massive human beings. You will let Doc see my vagina if he needs to!"

"Uh...yea, okay baby...sorry, of course," he said looking at his wife. Doc just grinned, knowing that Grace and Ghost had the same conversation when she was pregnant.

"OOOOOOOOOHHHHHHH Doc now!" yelled Gabi. "They're coming now!"

Doc covered her legs with a sheet and sure enough one beautiful head was already peeking out at him. Quickly donning gloves, he set down on the stool and spoke softly to her.

"Okay Gabi, next contraction go head and push honey," he said. She nodded, while Zulu held her shoulders up, she gripped behind her knees and pushed. "That's it honey...that's it...we've got a head full of blonde hair."

"Oh shit..." said Zulu looking down, "...blonde..." Gabi tried to smile, but just couldn't, she was in too much pain. She suspected that her color gene mutation was strong and the babies would carry it, she just hoped something about the twins would look like their daddy.

"Here comes another honey," said Doc, "push." She let out a wild scream as the next push came, breathing rapidly, screaming Quin's name. Quin wasn't sure if it was in love or anger, but right now he didn't care.

"Oh God...Quin I can't," she cried.

"Yes, you can Angel eyes," he said kissing her forehead. "You're the most amazing woman in the world, you can do this." Grace held her hand on the other side while Darby stood at Doc's shoulder.

"You can do this Gabi," said Grace. "We're here for your honey."

"Oh God...another..." She screamed at the same time a little tiny voice screamed out.

"You've got yourself a boy...a very...big...boy," said Doc grinning. There it is...what they got from their daddy, thought Gabi.

"Oh my God...oh my God baby look...he's blonde like you but..."

"Hung like you?" said Whiskey from the doorway.

"Shut up," said Zulu smiling at his friend, but he proudly nodded. "He's darker skinned...caramel colored." Gabi nodded as the wave of another contraction hit her.

"Okay honey...one more," said Doc. The second baby just wanted the hell out of there. He came all at once, with one big push looking just like his brother. "Identical...I think they're identical."

Gabi cried looking at her sons laying in her husband's arms. She lay her head back, sweat dripping from her brow as Grace wiped her face.

"You did so good Gabi," said Grace kissing her cheek. Darby patted her leg, smiling up at her.

"Almost there honey," said Darby. "Let Doc get the after-birth and get you cleaned up." She nodded and let Doc do his thing while she watched her husband with their sons. They were enormous babies.

"Let me weigh them," said Grace taking one from daddy's arms. "Oh wow…eight pounds two ounces, twenty-three inches long."

"Shit and that's just one," said Hawk smiling. Grace took the second little boy, although little was relative.

"Okay…seven pounds twelve ounces…twenty-two inches long."

"Damn," said Eagle, "we weren't anywhere near that big."

"Yea but look at the size of him," said Hawk pointing to Zulu. Zulu didn't even bother to give them any shit. He had two healthy baby boys and his beautiful wife looked amazing. Just as he was about to lay one down, he opened his eyes.

"Oh hell…he has your eyes only…I think they're violet," he said looking at Gabi. "Blonde hair, violet eyes, and caramel skin…shit they're gonna be pretty." Gabi laughed nodding with a tear in her eye.

When their second son opened his eyes, it was the same thing. Violet eyes.

"Have you thought of names?" asked Darby.

"Yea," said Zulu. "This little guy is Wade Eric Slater and this one…this little man is Tyler Gunner Slater." Gabi smiled at the four men who were the namesakes of their sons and noticed that they all had tears in their eyes.

"Damn brother," said Ghost.

"Yea...like give a guy a warning asshole," said Gunner.

"No shit," said Whiskey. Tango only nodded, swallowing hard. In the doorway was George holding Calla. She smiled at Darby and then looked to see two babies.

"Do you want to meet the babies Calla?" asked Gabi. She nodded walking slowly toward Zulu who was seated next to his wife.

"You have to be quiet uncle Zulu," she whispered. "Babies don't like loud noises so be careful when you walk." Laughter was heard around the room and Zulu nodded in a serious manner.

"What do you think?" asked Zulu.

"They're so pretty," she said touching their hair sweetly. She turned to Gunner, Darby in his arms smiling at the happy couple. "When you have a baby can you make sure we get two?"

CHAPTER THIRTY

Doc prepared well for the potential of a birth at the complex. He had everything that was needed, testing the babies right away and making sure Gabi was comfortable. Three hours later, the obstetrician had made her visit and confirmed that they didn't need her or the hospital, Doc had done an excellent job. She agreed that Gabi would be far more comfortable in her own home and approved Zulu moving them.

Hawk and Eagle insisted on carrying the babies to their new home, all the while telling them the fun things they would get to do as twins. Zulu couldn't help but smile since his twins were only hours old and they were already talking about how the boys could pick up girls and then switch if they didn't like the one they originally picked. Gabi turned looking at the men behind her, those eyes boring holes into them.

"I'd really appreciate it if you didn't teach my sons to be man whores," said Gabi.

"Hey...I'm offended," said Hawk feigning hurt. "I'm just teaching them how to get the most out of life, that's all." She just grinned as they stepped inside and got settled. Zulu took the babies from the guys and lay them in their basinets, which he realized they would outgrow fast.

"Let us know if you need anything man," said Eagle. "We're off to the bookstore again. If you hear a loud 'boom' just tell those two amazing babies stories about us."

"Not funny asshole," said Zulu. "Don't do anything stupid." They both nodded and headed back to meet the rest of the men. Gunner pulled Darby and Calla in for hugs and kisses, telling them he'd be home later.

"I'll be waiting," said Darby, "in nothing at all...just a mouth ready for you." She kissed his lips smiling and he growled, adjusting himself.

Gunner drove with Tango and Razor, while Eagle, Hawk, Ice, and Axe took another vehicle. As they approached the bookstore, they looked up and down the street to be sure it was empty or at least as empty as their little town could be. In the attic, they lit battery operated lights around the space for a better visual and carefully lifted the boxes one at a time, forming a human chain to get them downstairs.

With the first box safely settled on Darby's kitchen counter top, Razor removed the lid and sure enough there were twenty-four sticks of dynamite laying peacefully...for now, in the box. Picking up the first one, he delicately removed the cap and disconnected the fuse. Razor noticed crystals formed at the bottom of the box and let out a long sigh.

"What?" asked Gunner.

"The crystals at the bottom indicate that the nitro is probably old, but that means everything is more sensitive to motion, friction, and heat. I think our best bet is to get all this shit loaded, take it out somewhere away from everyone and just blow it."

"Fuck...okay...one box at a time," said Gunner. Forming their human chain they carried one box at a time down from the attic, loading it in the SUVs. Gunner locked the bookstore once more, knowing they would be back again tomorrow. "Let's head toward the old quarry at the northeast of town."

Tango nodded as he drove as slowly as possible without drawing attention to them. As the main roads turned into back, gravel roads, he cursed every time they hit a pothole, and prayed they would make it in one piece. Taking the winding drive down into the quarry, they carefully unloaded the boxes, stacking them together. Gunner instructed that they all drive back up to the edge of the quarry away from the explosion.

"Hawk? Eagle? Get your MRAD's ready." Both men nodded, pulling out their long-range sniper rifles. "Nothing fancy boys, just one shot each at the same time if possible."

Eagle lay on his stomach next to his brother, both stretching out, their rifles propped before them. Hawk turned his ball cap backwards as Razor shone a spotlight on the grouping of boxes. He looked at his brother and nodded.

"One...two...*thwap!*" The explosion was deafening as the cases of dynamite blew fragments of dirt and rock into the air, the fiery ball lighting up the night sky; the ground rumbled beneath them. Gunner's phone vibrated and he answered.

"Please tell me that was your doing, but not you," said Ghost. Gunner smiled.

"It was us brother. We got it all and brought it to the quarry. Can't believe you felt that shit," he said smiling at the others.

"The whole damn house shook man. You guys, okay?" asked Ghost.

"We're okay brother, headed home now." Gunner nodded as they loaded up and headed back to the compound. Inside the gates, he thanked each man and told them they would meet again in the morning at eight. As he stepped through his front door, he smiled at the sleeping form of his soon-to-be wife and their daughter curled on top of her.

Lifting Calla easily, he took her upstairs and tucked her in bed, then returned to lift Darby in his arms. She curled her arms around his neck and took a deep breath, inhaling the scent she knew was her man. Her lips trailed up his neck and he growled as he felt himself harden.

Laying her in their bed, he pulled the sheet over her and she barely opened her eyes, holding her hands out.

"Wait...I was going to..." He kissed her, stopping her from speaking further.

"I'm gonna shower baby, we're both tired. All I want to do is hold you tonight, okay?" She sat up and looked at him.

"Are you okay? Did everything go okay?" she said panicked.

"Everything is good beautiful...I promise. Let me just hold my woman tonight, okay?" She nodded as he showered and then crawled in beside her. True to his word, he pulled her close to his body and just held her tightly against him. Just her and him, together for tonight.

Tomorrow might be another story.

CHAPTER THIRTY-ONE

Zulu and Gabi were noticeably missing from breakfast as expected, but the rest of the team was there along with Darby and Calla. As always, she picked the seat next to her favorite uncle, Tango. She spoke in an animated fashion about her role as Betsy Ross and how important it was to make sure she got all her lines right. She was also very excited at having white hair for the role, although Tango wanted to question the accuracy of that. Instead, he nodded looking at her with a serious expression, as if hanging on her every word.

"Whatcha lookin' at beautiful?" asked Gunner, kissing Darby's cheek.

"Tango and Calla. He's really good with kids. I hope he and Taylor figure out that they're right for one another and do something about it. She's really special." Gunner smiled at his woman and nodded.

"I think we should let nature take its course baby. Don't interfere," he grinned. She nodded but was already thinking of ways to ensure their day at the Fourth of July picnic would be eventful. "Let's go boys, we gotta drop Calla at school."

"Bye mommy!" she said waving her little hand. Darby couldn't help but shake her head at the sight of her happy little girl. She'd always been cheery, with a sweet disposition, but being here among all these men and especially Gunner, Tango and George, it was as if she'd transformed overnight. Gunner kissed his woman and left the room with the others.

As they pulled in front of the bookstore, Gunner and Tango walked toward the school, each holding one of Calla's small hands.

"If people didn't know us, they'd think Calla has two daddies," whispered Tango. Gunner chuckled at that and thought about how they looked, two big, burly, leather-clad men with a little girl. Tango waited as Gunner took Calla inside, appearing a few minutes later ready to start work at the store.

As they walked past the coffee shop, Tango peered inside to see Taylor working hard.

"Get your coffee brother," said Gunner grinning. "Meet us in the attic." He nodded and opened the door to a smiling Taylor. He waited in line patiently, realizing she was busier than usual, most likely due to the upcoming holiday.

"Good morning Tango," she said quietly.

"Morning Taylor. Six coffee's this morning and a dozen pastries, whatever you have the most of," he grinned. Tango didn't need the pastries, they'd all eaten at the club before they left. George would have their hides if he knew they'd eaten a huge breakfast and then come here to eat pastries, but he just couldn't help himself. Taylor hurriedly filled his order and handed it to him.

"Hey Tango...there was a man in here earlier asking when the bookstore would be open."

"Okay...is that unusual?" he asked.

"No...it's just this guy didn't really look like he was interested in books. He kept asking about the former owner, if he had any friends or family in the area." That got Tango's attention. Someone was snooping and they needed to get their shit straight before anyone knew they'd found the boxes.

"Thanks Taylor...see ya at lunch." She smiled and nodded, waving as he left. Back in the bookstore he went upstairs to join the other guys. Not touching the blocks of cocaine, they pulled the suitcases down and lay them out on the counters and tables. There were nine in all, all the same style of case, all locked tight.

"Do you think they're rigged?" asked Gunner looking at Razor.

"Don't think so…these are designed to withstand heat, water, just about anything. I'd say there was drugs in them, except all the drugs are just laying about in the attic." Gunner nodded as Razor popped the latches on the first case, carefully opening it.

"It's an escape case," whispered Gunner. The other men looked at him with questioning eyes. "We saw these a lot in South America. The drug lords would have a case stashed with passports, cash, fake papers, sometimes jewelry or drugs. Look…there are five passports in here waiting for pictures."

The men looked through the case and sure enough it was as if it were a do-it-yourself escape case, just waiting to insert names and photos on the documents.

"My guess is one of the other suitcases is already prepared for someone," said Gunner. "Let's get to opening brothers." They opened each case carefully examining the contents, finding that each was the same as the first. Finally, at the last one, Gunner looked at the others crossing his fingers. He opened the case and took out the passports.

"Fuuuucccckkkk!" he growled. Tango and Hawk looked over his shoulder and immediately took a step back. Eagle and Ice stepped forward and looked down, then Hawk, Axe, and last was Razor.

"Son-of-a-bitch."

"My sentiments exactly," said Gunner taking out his phone. "Ghost? Yea brother you need to get down to the bookstore to see this." The men shut the case and stacked the blank ones against the wall, waiting for Ghost. They would destroy the blanks, but this one...this one might need some support. If Javier Ascencio was connected to the individual indicated in this case, they needed to make sure everything was handled perfectly.

"What do we do about Javier?" asked Hawk. "We promised him the case today...we can't give this shit to him."

"I know that," said Gunner through clenched teeth. "Let's just wait for Ghost." Fifteen minutes later, they heard the rumbling roar of motorcycles as Ghost, Whiskey, and Doc pulled up. Meeting them downstairs with the case in hand, the three men looked at the faces of their teammates.

"Fuck...who died?" asked Whiskey. Gunner set the case on the counter, turning it toward the three men, then opened it.

Ghost looked into the case, picking up the passports and documents, then looking up at the men again. There was probably a hundred thousand in cash along with a stack of bearer bonds. He let out a slow whistle.

"Is this a fucking joke?" asked Whiskey with a hint of disgust.

"No fucking joke brother. Assad Bashiir."

"The Assad Bashiir who ordered the deaths of those twelve little girls?" asked Doc. "The same fucker who called for our exit from the unit. We all knew that fucker was behind those killings, now he's trying to get here to the states?" Gunner took out his phone on a hunch.

"Ace? Brother...I need the whereabouts of Assad Bashiir...yea...that Assad Bashiir." He waited patiently listening to the clicking of keys in the background. No one said a word, no one seemed to breathe. "Fuck. He's here...already in the U.S. allegedly working as a diplomat with the U.N. That fucker is trying to get the paperwork to stay and go underground."

"He's going to create a terrorist network right here," said Whiskey looking at Gunner.

"Not if we have anything to say about it."

"We can't turn this case over to Javier," said Razor. "But if we don't, he's going to rip this place apart and target Darby and Calla."

"What if we set a trap for him?" said Hawk. "Let him meet those two idiots somewhere claiming they have the suitcase, take Javier and then find where Assad is located."

"Okay," said Ghost. "It's your plan Gunner. Darby and Calla are yours, and protected by us brother, but you call the rules on this. What do you want to do?"

Gunner let out a long slow breath walking around the bookstore, thinking about the fact that it was Darby's dream. He couldn't destroy the bookstore; besides it would destroy the coffee shop next door as well.

"We arrange to meet them like you suggested. We'll let Tweedle Dee and Tweedle Dumb make the call to Javier and nab him. Have them meet us at the quarry where we were last night. It's empty, no one around for miles."

"I'll head back to the compound and get the two fucks to make the call," said Whiskey.

"How do you want to handle this with Darby?" asked Ghost.

"I'm not going to tell her what we found, just that it wasn't something she would want in her home. I think if we can get this done with Javier, then get the DEA in to remove the drugs, we'll be okay." The men all nodded. "I'm gonna pick up Calla and then we can head back. Let's get Whiskey to arrange the meet for tomorrow at noon."

"Fucking Assad Bashiir," said Ghost. Gunner looked up at him and back at Razor, Tango, and Doc who were part of the original team along with Whiskey and Zulu. "What?"

"Admiral Crossing? He still alive and active?" asked Gunner.

"I think so...alive anyway," said Ghost.

"Think he would tell us what's going on with this guy?" Ghost grinned at his friend and teammate nodding. Gunner nodded in return

"Time for him to pay us back."

CHAPTER THIRTY-TWO

The following morning, the men sat around the big conference table staring at the screen and the face of Admiral Mike Crossing. Crossing had been the man to originally form their Special Forces team, assigning most of the missions and ensuring they always had what they'd needed. When the shit with the little girls went down in Somalia, he was the only one on the panel who fought for them.

In the end though, he was getting push back from the higher-ups, as well as the local government and tribes. It was bullshit all the way, but they'd appreciated that he stuck his neck out for them all, allowing them to retire.

"Admiral, it's good to see you," said Ghost.

"Don't lie Ghost, it's not becoming of a man your age. I'm probably the last person any of you wanted to see, although I see some faces I don't know who still might hold out a positive opinion of my ancient ass."

"Yes sir, we have a different sort of team now. The original guys and I formed a club, a motorcycle club and we help people who need it.

We also own a bar and restaurant and a kick-ass custom car and motorcycle shop."

"Damn! You boys have done well for yourselves," he said smiling. His face sobered and he linked his fingers in front of him. "I'm damned sorry the way things ended for you boys. It was fucked up all the way."

"That's sort of why we're calling sir."

"No sirs anymore Gunner...I'm just Mike."

"Yes...ummm okay Mike, I'll give it a try," he grinned. "Assad Bashiir." The old man on the screen let out a low slow whistle staring at the screen.

"You really know how to make a man's heart stop don't you Gunner?" His expression was grave and serious, staring at the men. "What do you want to know?"

"Why is he here in the U.S. working as a diplomat?" asked Ghost.

"A few years ago, he came forward denouncing all the crimes in his country, admitting that he'd been a part of that at one time, but was now trying to improve his country, wanted it cleaned up. He claimed that he wanted all the drug lords gone, the tribal lords who were stealing children, forcing boys to serve in the military...everything. He even invested millions of his own money in trying to rebuild villages."

"You mean the millions he stole from the very people he's claiming to protect?" asked Whiskey.

"Yep...that would be those millions," grinned Mike. "He tried running for political office but was defeated. Now he's trying a new tactic. He thinks by playing nice with the U.N., they'll allow him permanent residency here in the U.S. with full diplomatic immunity. I think he wants to form his own terrorist network here and get a piece of what the other terrorist networks already claim to own."

"He's already doing it," said Gunner. Mike's face went blank as he sat back in his big leather chair. "We found documentation that he's trying to buy passports and documentation, giving him a U.S., Canadian, Mexican, and British passport. All the countries he would need to travel in and out of to get support, money, drugs, troops...anything and everything he would need."

"Fucking hell," the older man muttered. "You're supposed to be retired you know?"

"Believe me, we know sir. We need to stop Bashiir, but we may need help further up the chain than what we can reach. It's a long story, but we've found several cases that are basically ready-made escape cases, along with several hundred kilos of cocaine."

"I'll be damned. You boys really aren't retired, are you?" he smirked.

"We're trying sir, I promise you."

"Let me see what I can find out on my end," he said to the screen. "I would suggest in the meantime you don't do anything."

"One more thing Mike," said Ghost. "Ever hear of a guy by the name of Javier Ascencio?"

"Yep, he's a mean one him. Worked for Castillo down in Juarez for a while kidnapping for ransom, drugs, trafficking...his hands were in everything. DEA tried to take him down a few times and then lost track of him. Why?"

"We may know where he is," said Gunner between clenched teeth.

"Piece of advice then?" said Mike. Gunner and the rest of the team nodded. "Lock down everything you value. If you don't, he'll find a way to get to it."

CHAPTER THIRTY-THREE

Whiskey made the two men they were holding call Javier the day before, arranging the meet just as they'd asked for. Early the next morning, the men staked their spots around the quarry, with Eagle and Hawk finding a spot to have the man in their sights long range. Whiskey, Ghost, Razor, Axe, and Ice were scattered around the space concealed under cover of bushes or trees, their camouflage making them appear a part of the landscape.

Gunner and Tango, with baseball caps pulled down, would arrive in the same truck the two men had used, keeping a distance until Javier pulled in. Waiting for the other vehicle, Gunner checked and rechecked his weapons.

"So, how's Taylor doing?" asked Gunner with a grin.

"Shut up," smirked Tango. "She's...she's Taylor brother. I thought she was so young, but it turns out she's only a few years younger than me. She looks like she's maybe twenty-two with all those crazy blonde curls and big blue eyes."

"Big blue eyes, huh?" said Gunner smiling.

"Shut the fuck up," growled Tango. "Yea...big blue eyes. She's just...different brother. Different from the women I usually hook up with, because fucking sure I never date anyone. I actually want to date her...see where it goes."

"I'm glad for you brother. When you know you know. It's that simple. When I saw Darby walk into the gym that day, I damned near came in my shorts."

"TMI," said Tango with a disgusted face.

"What the fuck ever. She was just it...everything about her. I just knew man and I suspect you're feeling the same shit with Taylor." Tango nodded. "Besides, think how cute your couple name will be...Taygo."

"You say that again and I'm revoking your man card," said Tango. He looked up to see a white van driving straight toward them. Pulling his cap down further, he nodded to Gunner who did the same, slinking in the seat to appear smaller.

The van pulled up but just sat parked, with no one moving, no one getting out. Finally, a man stepped around the side door, something concealed in his hand. He was tall, dark hair and eyes and definitely Hispanic.

"Get out," he called to the men in the truck. "I know who you are...get out." Gunner looked at Tango and nodded. In their ear, they heard Ghost.

"Don't do anything stupid, we have him in sight."

Gunner stood next to Tango at the hood of the truck staring at the man.

"You have something I want," he said grinning.

"Sorry man, don't know what you mean," said Gunner shrugging. "I just want you to back off the bookstore lady."

"I think you do have something for me gringo. You see I'm not as stupid as my men that you so easily took down. I wasn't indisposed these past few days...I was watching...watching and waiting. I know you found dynamite, I know you found the drugs, and I know you found the cases."

"So, you know...now we know you want it...problem is you won't get it," said Gunner. He grinned at both men with his hand on the sliding side door.

"Oh...I think I will," he said pushing the door back. Lying in the back of the van was Calla and Taylor, both strapped with suicide vests, their mouths taped shut with duct tape. Gunner started to step forward, but the man held up a firing switch.

"Uh...uh...uh," he said smiling. "You take one step toward me, you even think about allowing those men to shoot at me, they will be dead before the bullet hits." Tango stared into the eyes of Taylor, tears streaking her face, but she tried to get closer to Calla, comforting the little girl.

"Take the tape off the girl, she's too little to know to breathe through her nose," said Gunner.

"Oh...you mean your soon-to-be daughter?" he said grinning. "You see I know everything...every...thing. I will take the tape off but if she cries, I will place it back on." Gunner nodded as he pulled the tape roughly from her mouth. She gasped for air, her tears falling more freely down her face.

"Daddy...uncle Tango..." she cried.

"It's okay baby, daddy and uncle Tango are going to get you," he said trying to calm the little girl.

"That's right," said Javier, "daddy and uncle Tango are going to give Mr. Javier everything he's asked for and then...maybe...they can have you back in little tiny pieces."

"You touch them," said Tango staring at Taylor, her big blue eyes wet with tears, "you lay one finger, disturb one hair on their heads and I'll fucking kill you."

"Such language in front of the child. You do realize that I could have them sold and, on a ship, before you two even know where I've taken them. You see I have endless resources, endless, which is why Bashiir contacted me. The problem is that idiot at the shipping store went and died on me without telling me where everything was stashed. Then that pretty woman of yours buys the building and I can't get in without creating an issue."

"So, here's what's going to happen. You're going to bring the drugs, the cases, and the dynamite to me by noon tomorrow or they're both dead."

"The dynamite was blown the other night...it was unstable," said Gunner. Javier nodded.

"Fine…replace it with C4. We both know you have access to it. Bring an equal number of blocks of C4 along with the cases and the drugs." He started to round the van then turned to the two men. "If you try to follow me, if you even think about coming after me…well, it would be such a shame to let a buyer have these two beauties."

Gunner watched as the van drove away and collapsed to his knees, Tango rushing to his side. He was struggling to get enough air in his lungs, his hand shaking violently at his sides.

"Brother…we have to go…we have to find them," said Tango.

"No…we can't risk them…we can't risk either of them," he said as the other men came running toward them. "Fuck." He cried.

"We'll find them," said Ghost. "We'll find them."

"Hey…does anyone want to know where the van is heading?"

It was the voice of the ever-faithful Ace.

"You know where he's going?" said Gunner into his mouthpiece.

"Uh yea…that's what you guys pay me for. I linked into his phone and GPS while he was chatting with you guys. He's about ten miles north, headed to the West Virginia border."

"Keep tracking him Ace...we're going to follow at a distance but let us know when he stops," said Ghost. "And Ace...call Mike and see if we can link to a satellite."

"I don't really need his permission...I can just make that happen."

"I love you, you freaking geek!" yelled Gunner. "And Ace? Don't tell the girls anything right now, okay?"

"I might be a geek, but I'm not stupid. Get going."

"Let's go," said Gunner staring at Tango, "let's bring our girls home."

CHAPTER THIRTY-FOUR

Darby held one of the twins, she wasn't even sure which one, rocking him slowly in her arms humming a soft sweet lullaby she used to sing to Calla. Gabi held the other to her breast feeding him, as he hungrily sucked and pulled her sensitive nipples.

"I don't know how long I'm going to be able to do this," she winced. "These two must have taken lessons from their daddy because this shit hurts." Darby smiled at her.

"I didn't breast feed, I bottle-fed. I think I was struggling so much with just being pregnant and Clint throwing me aside I wasn't really as into having Calla as a new mother should be."

"Honey, there is no rule book for how new moms should behave. Some of us have post-partum depression, some don't; some are instant nurturers, others aren't." Darby nodded at the other woman, then looked back down at the striking combination of blonde hair and caramel skin on the boy in her arms.

"They're going to be stunning little boys Gabi," she grinned at the other woman.

"Yea, I was a little worried about their coloring while I was pregnant. My genes are very unusual and strong. Even with the contrast between Quin and I, I knew that mine would win out as the dominant. I just didn't expect violet eyes."

"I wonder where the guys are?" asked Darby looking around for a clock. "They should have picked up Calla and been home by now." Gabi shrugged.

"You know them, they probably stopped for ice cream and bought her a pony or something ridiculous," she laughed. "Although I have to tell you, it's so sweet to watch those big men hover over her and dote on her, especially Tango."

"I know," she said nodding. "I was really worried about all these men around her, but it seems she's sweet-talked all of them. Probably something I need to keep an eye as she becomes a teenager."

Gabi laughed and then looked down at her sleeping son. Slowly removing her nipple from his mouth, she winced again.

"Oh honey...it's really red. Maybe you should call your doctor. This might not be the route for you," said Darby empathizing and feeling the woman's' pain.

"I know…I know…I just hoped to be able to do this for a while, but it's only been a few days and I'm already praying for it to stop. I know they say breast is best, but those people didn't have two babies latching on like bionic sucking machines." Darby looked down at her phone, seeing the number for the daycare ringing in.

"Hello?"

"Is this Darby Greer?" asked the woman in a frantic voice.

"Yes…what's wrong?"

"Ms. Greer, this is Mrs. Drummond from your daughters' school."

"Yes…what's happened? What's wrong?"

"I…I left my nieces in charge this morning and when I returned, I noticed Calla was gone. They said…they said a man claiming to be here uncle came by to get her, but when I looked at our video footage, it wasn't the usual men that come to get her."

"Oh my God! Call the police!"

"NO!" yelled Gabi. "No…not yet. Call Gunner first Darby…please trust me in this. Call Gunner."

"Mrs. Drummond don't do anything. I'm going to call my husband," she said without thinking. Clicking end on the call, she quickly dialed Gunner. "Gunner? Calla…"

"I know baby…I know, and I need you to trust me. We're following the man that has her right now." Darby felt herself sway and lowered herself to the floor before she hit it unwillingly. "Honey? Baby trust me…I'll get her back."

"Oh God…" she said quietly. Gabi took the phone from her.

"Gunner? This is Gabi…what the hell is happening?" She listened as Gunner relayed as much of the information as he was willing, nodding her head as she lay down the twins. "Keep us informed Gunner."

"Wh-what's happening? What's going on Gabi?"

"Honey listen to me, those men that tore apart your store took Calla and Taylor. Gunner and the boys are already on their tail. They will find them, and they will bring them home honey, we just have to be patient."

"Patient? That's my only child Gabi! That's my…my life…my…oh God what have I done? I thought I could have it all with Gunner…I thought I was safe. I should have known…I should have…"

"Darby! Stop!" yelled Grace coming through the front door hearing the last of her tirade. "Stop right now. You know that Gunner will lay down his life to bring that child back to you. Listen to me Darby. These men do not fail. They are highly trained, highly skilled warriors."

"Ex-warriors," said Darby staring at the older woman. "They're not active duty any longer Grace."

"Honey you don't get it. These men are never ex-anything. They keep in peak physical form and they know what the hell they're doing. You need to keep a cool head and know that Gunner will do anything to bring that little girl back to you." Darby nodded, tears streaming down her face.

"Oh God...oh God what if Gunner or one of the others' gets hurt?" she cried.

"They know the risks Darby," said Gabi. "All of them know the risks they're taking by doing this and they take those risks with eyes wide open."

"What do we do?" she whispered almost to herself.

"We wait..." The front door opened, and Zulu and a distinguished older gentleman walked in the door.

"We wait and keep you safe," said the older man. "Ladies, I'm Admiral Mike Crossing, United States Navy retired. I'm doing everything in my power to help those men out there and those two girls. You can rest assured we will get them back."

"And if you don't get them back?" asked Darby.

"I can't believe any other outcome is possible ma'am. It's the only viable end with those men out there."

"From your lips to Gods' ears."

CHAPTER THIRTY-FIVE

They just stopped about four miles ahead of you guys...took a right turn toward a large farmhouse. Satellite shows him taking the girls inside.

"We're on it," said Ghost from the back of the SUV. "What kind of cover do we have Ace?"

Lots of trees on the surrounding property...it's getting close to dusk so that could play in your favor. Ghost you guys need to move fast...I see three more black SUV's approaching from the south...probably ten or eleven miles back but that many vehicles like that in this part of West Virginia can't be good.

"Fuck!" yelled Gunner.

"Easy brother," said Tango from the seat beside him. "We're going to get them out."

"Park at the tree line," said Ghost. "Let Hawk and Eagle do some recon, make sure there aren't sensors." Gunner nodded, pulling into the trees. Hawk immediately leapt out of the second vehicle with his brother and wound their way through the threes, searching up and down for trip wires or sensors that would alert the man in the house to their presence.

"Nothing," said Hawk in their earpieces.

"Slowly," said Ghost. "Like any other fucking mission, we've ever been on. We take it slow and easy. No fuck ups. Everyone goes home...everyone." Gunner and Tango both swallowed, nodding. The problem for both of them was that on no other mission had the stakes been so high.

Ghost...Admiral Crossing says that house has a basement...it was used as a drug safehouse about ten years ago and the feds found it and then abandoned it...might even have an escape tunnel.

"Fuck! Move...move!" Gunner's big boot hit the door and he looked across the room to see Calla seated in a big chair, her suicide vest now connected to a timer.

"Oh damn," he whispered.

"Let me," said Razor kneeling in front of her. He gently pulled off the tape and smiled at her. "It's okay sweet girl...Uncle Razor is going to get this off of you."

"I knew you'd come daddy," she hiccupped. "I...I peed my pants...the bad man wouldn't let me go to the bathroom."

"It's okay sweet baby," said Gunner kneeling next to Razor. "You just sit still and let uncle Razor get this thing off you, okay?" She nodded but didn't move as Razor talked more to himself than anyone else.

"Basic wiring...timer...detonator...I've done a million of these...a million," he said smiling up at Calla. It was as if the little girl could sense his anxiety.

"I love you uncle Razor."

"I love you too honey," he said cutting the first wire with the last breath expelling from his lungs. The timer stopped and he shuddered with relief. Next, he cut the detonator wire and then sliced through the tape holding it to her tiny body. Lifting it off, he handed it back to Hawk who took it outside. Calla jumped into Gunner's arms, squeezing his neck.

"Oh baby..." he sobbed, "...daddy was so worried about you. I'm so sorry Calla...I'm so sorry I wasn't there."

"I knew you'd come daddy...I knew it...you're my superhero. The bad man told Miss Jenny that he was my uncle. I knew he wasn't, but he had Miss Taylor and I knew he was gonna hurt her." He smiled down at the little girl, kissing her face.

"You're such a brave little girl, Calla. Let's go outside and call mama, okay?"

"Okay," she said bouncing her head up and down. "Find Taylor daddy, the bad man hit her." Razor took off through the house trying to find Tango and the others as Gunner took Calla outside. Sitting in the backseat of the SUV, he dialed Darby's number, placing the phone on video view so that she could see her daughter was fine.

"Gunner! Oh God…Calla…baby, are you okay?" she asked frantically.

"I'm fine mommy. Daddy rescued me but I had a accident…I had to go bad and the man wouldn't let me go in the potty."

"Oh, baby it's okay…it's all okay. You and daddy just come home as fast as you can so I can hug you, okay?"

"Okay mommy," she said handing the phone back to Gunner, but never letting go of his neck.

"We'll be home soon Darby. Baby…baby I'm so s-sorry," he choked out.

"It's okay," she said seeing the emotion coming from him. "It's alright…really. This wasn't your fault. I don't know what I would have done if you hadn't been here Gunner. I just need my family back

together, okay?" He nodded and disconnected the call.

"Can we go home daddy?"

"As soon as we find Taylor baby...as soon as we find Taylor."

CHAPTER THIRTY-SIX

"Get up!" he growled at her has he pulled her hair, trying to lift her to her feet. He slapped her again, then punched her lower pelvic area causing her to urinate herself. She cried out, doubling over again.

"You will fucking get up or I will put a bullet in your brain," he said, spittle flying into her face. He pulled the tape from her mouth.

"Please...please I can't...I'm hurting," she cried.

"Shut the fuck up and get moving," he said yanking on her arm. When she stumbled again, he turned and slammed his fist into her face. Taylor fell back against the floor of the wet tunnel, darkness enveloping her. "Get up cunt!"

Taylor heard him but couldn't gain any sense of what was up or down, her face filled with pain, blood oozing from her nose and mouth.

"Touch her again and you die mother-fucker," said Tango staring down the man hovering over Taylor. "I have three guns pointed at your greasy ass. You have nowhere left to escape to. Let her go."

"You forget I hold all the cards here," he said grinning with the switch in his hand. "You kill me, she dies."

"You kill her...we all die," said Tango. "Let her go and you walk away." Javier eyed the man carefully. There weren't a lot of options here. They were truly at a standoff. If he didn't let the girl go, he was dead either by the explosives in her vest or by one of the bullets aimed at his head.

"How do I know you'll let me walk?" he asked staring Tango down.

"Because unlike you I have a soul and a conscience. I want the woman to live. You've already lost the little girl, she's safe," he said taking another step closer. Javier took a step back, Taylor still lying at his feet writhing in pain, moaning.

"I don't think so," he said smiling. He should have done what the man asked, should have taken the deal to run. He saw it a fraction too late, the muzzle blast of the silencer on a rifle. He saw it before he felt it, the top of half of his hand flew into the air, the fingers instinctively opening. Looking at the bloody palm, with no fingers attached he started to scream, but not before a second bullet hit him square between the eyes.

Tango rushed to scoop Taylor in his arms as she moaned against his body, writhing in pain. She tried to push him away, but he held strong, pulling her closer to his body.

"It's okay honey...we've got you," he said racing back toward the house. In the waning evening light, they noticed that her vest wasn't on a timer and Razor made quick work of removing it as well, but it was her bloodied and battered face that gave them all pause.

Boys you've got about three minutes to get the hell out of there before you have company.

"Let's get her to Gabi," said Gunner. "Hawk? Call Gabi and Doc, let them know we're comin' in hot with Taylor."

Tango held onto Taylor in the backseat of the second SUV, trying to keep her from Calla's eyes. He whispered sweet things in her ear, telling her all would be okay, but the entire time hating himself for not getting to her quicker.

"You're gonna be just fine honey...you have to be. We have a date next weekend and I'm gonna hold you to it," he said kissing her forehead.

As they pulled into the compound, Doc raced out helping Tango with Taylor.

"Get her upstairs to Gabi," he yelled, taking one look at the blood and the shape of her nose. Gunner watched them carry Taylor away and then turned to see Darby racing toward him. She flung herself into his open arm, the other still holding tight to Calla, not willing to set her down.

"Mommy!" she yelled. "Mommy I'm back from an adventure."

"Yes, my sweet baby...yes you are!" she said with tear-filled eyes.

"I'm so..." Darby shook her head and swallowed.

"Don't. I have my daughter because of you. You're both uninjured, unharmed. This will be an adventure she tells, not a story of terror. I thought I couldn't love you any more Gunner...but I was wrong. I love you so much I know now I wouldn't survive if you didn't come home to me every night."

"You won't ever have to worry about that baby. I will always come home to you. You are my home Darby...you and Calla are my home." She nodded, kissing him once again.

"Let's get this one cleaned up and then come back to check on Taylor," he said. Darby nodded, still tucked safely beneath his arm, while he held firmly to Calla with the other. They were going to be okay, but the question was, would Taylor be alright.

CHAPTER THIRTY-SEVEN

"Called the DEA," said Zulu. "They're on the way to meet Axe and Ice at the bookstore to get the drugs out of there. Said they'd been watching Javier knowing he had a connection to Assad. They weren't sure what they were doing, but knew it wasn't good."

"Fuckers could have given us a heads up," growled Whiskey. Gunner walked in to see them all seated at the big table.

"What's the word on Taylor?" he asked right away.

"Nothing yet," said Zulu. "Angel eyes is up there with Doc now. Just telling them that Ice and Axe are meeting the drug boys at the store to get rid of the packages." Gunner nodded looking at the others.

"I...I owe you all a debt...thank you," he said staring at them.

"What the fuck Gunner?" said Whiskey. "We're brothers' man...fucking brothers. It's what we do. We helped when Grace needed it and Ghost was falling fast; we helped when Doc and Bree needed it; you all helped when Kat needed it; we helped Zulu and Angel eyes and we fucking helped you and Darby. We're a family man...you know that. But even if we weren't, we would have never allowed that man to touch those girls." Gunner nodded, but then sat in the closest chair and sobbed.

He felt the strong hands of his brothers against his shoulders and finally looked up, wiping the tears from his face.

"She thought it was a fucking adventure," he laughed. "Said she knew we would find her even though the bad man said we wouldn't. Fucking innocent child man...*my* innocent child."

"I know brother," said Zulu. "Believe me, all I could think about was if someone tried to take Wade or Tyler...brother I'm not sure any of you could control the rage that was building in me, just with the thought of it." Ghost nodded, tugging at his beard.

"Same brother. I kept thinking if he had lain his hands on JT; I don't know if I would've been thinking clearly to lead the team."

"Maybe we think about training for this," said Hawk. "I mean, you all seem to be getting married and poppin' out the kids. Maybe we think about this."

"What do you mean?" asked Gunner.

"I did some training with some fat cat corporate heads on evasion and tactical driving. They were all more concerned about keeping their kids safe, put guards on 'em twenty-four-seven. Not sure that's much of a life for a kid, but maybe we think of something else."

"The trackers," said Ace standing in the door. "We gave them to the girls...haven't given one yet to Darby, Taylor or Amanda, but maybe we should and maybe we should think about the kids. Do an ankle bracelet or something."

"Could you do that brother?" asked Zulu. Ace looked offended and then realized he was being sincere in his question.

"Oh...yea, I can make them any size, any shape...whatever we need." Ghost nodded as the phone rang.

"Yea Ice...fuck! Okay, call the sheriff and see what you can help with."

"What's wrong?" asked Gunner.

"The shops are both trashed. Javier must have had someone go in after he took the girls and tear the places apart. Looks like the bookstore was just books tossed, but the coffee shop is nearly totaled. Taylor's gonna be devastated."

"Fuck!" growled Gunner.

"We'll take care of it brother...together," said Zulu. He nodded, then looked up to see Doc standing in the doorway, his shirt bloody.

"Jesus," whispered Gunner. "H-how is she?"

"She's a fucking mess. I don't know how he did so much damage in such a short period of time. Her nose is broken, a few teeth knocked out, fractured eye socket, broken wrist, broken ribs, and her pelvis is bruised along with her bladder and uterus. Angel eyes was fucking awesome in there, but she's going to need some reconstructive surgery."

"What can we do?" asked Ghost.

"Nothin' right now. Gabi called for an ambulance to move her to a hospital. She needs to be under the care of a plastic surgeon and potentially a gynecologist. We spoke and she's agreed to tell them she was in an automobile wreck and we found her." Ghost nodded but hated like fuck that she was put in that position.

They heard the sounds of the ambulance and rushed out to greet it, helping to bring Taylor down the stairs. Tango refused to leave her side, holding her hand the entire way.

"I'm going with her," he said to Ghost who only nodded.

"Call us as soon as you know anything," he said quietly. Tango nodded, stepping into the back of the ambulance, latching onto her unbroken hand once again. They watched as it pulled out, lights and sirens going.

"Get some sleep everyone…"

"Ghost?" said Ace poking his head out. "You're not gonna believe this, but Assad Bashiir is calling in for you."

"What the ever-loving-fuck?" said Gunner staring at the faces around him.

"Let's take it in the conference room," he said to everyone as they piled back into the space. "Put it on speaker...hello."

"My old friend Master Chief Stanton." The heavily accented voice of Assad Bashiir came through the phone and every man in the room froze at the sound of his voice.

"I'm not your fucking friend Bashiir."

"You always did use such foul language. I've beaten you at every turn you know…you've never once beaten me, until today. Today…you found the girls, took my drugs and documents, and you killed my very best man. Consider us even."

"We're not fucking even close to even you piece of human waste," growled Ghost. "You killed hundreds of thousands of your own people, including those twelve little girls. We are far from even."

"You always were a bleeding heart just like the rest of the Americans. That's fine...but you won't win. I will be here...waiting for my next opportunity and of course with you now retired, there is not one thing you can do about it. You have the two girls...consider them my gift to you."

"We might be retired Bashiir but believe me we're not done. You're on our turf now...in our land and you fucking bet we will find you...and this time we will end you...permanently." Ghost heard the click of the line, ending the call and let out a long, slow breath.

"Go home...get some sleep," he said staring at everyone. "We'll meet tomorrow."

CHAPTER THIRTY-EIGHT

Gunner stood in the doorway of Calla's room watching her sleep. He ran the scenario through his head a million times, the look on her sweet face when Javier pulled the van door open; her tears streaking those perfect little cheeks. He couldn't breathe, couldn't think of anything except her. How was he going to do this? How was he going to keep her safe from the shit he knew was out there in the world?

He tried to walk in the other direction several times, but just couldn't. It was as if his feet were glued to the floor. He felt Darby's arms wrap around his waist from behind, her head laying against his back.

"When she was two," she said softly, "she contracted pneumonia. Her fevers were so high...I thought she was going to die. I had no health insurance and of course I couldn't find Clint anywhere. I finally didn't have a choice, I had to take her to the emergency room."

"They did the x-ray confirming it was pneumonia, gave us some antibiotics and sent us home. Except she wasn't getting better. She was on her third round of antibiotics before they figured out that she was immune to them. While we were sitting in the hospital...just her and I in that little room, she had a seizure from the fever."

Gunner turned her in his arms and held her close, kissing the top of her head. He could only imagine how afraid she must have been being alone with a child that young, sick and having seizures on top of all that.

"She was fine after that...they got her fever down but for a week I refused to let her sleep alone. Every time I closed my eyes, I thought she might have another seizure and I wouldn't be there to help her."

"What did you do?" he asked wiping the tears from his eyes.

"I did what every parent does...I lost some sleep and then I realized she was going to be okay. You can't watch her every second of the day Gunner...you just can't and it's going to get worse the older she gets. What are you going to do when she wants to have a sleep-over at a friends' house? Or the first time she goes to the movies with friends?"

"Follow her? Track her?" he said looking down at Darby's smiling face.

"I love that you're so protective over her Gunner, but you have to let her be a little girl too. I was terrified when I learned that she'd been taken, but I also knew that the bravest, kindest, most beautiful man in the world was out there rescuing her. You'll always be there to rescue her

Gunner. It's what a good father would do...and that's you...a good father."

He nodded looking at the sleeping, sweet face of Calla once more as Darby tugged his hand. He reluctantly followed and then stopped in the hallway.

"Just for tonight?" he begged. Darby smiled back at him and nodded. Gunner raced back to Calla's room and picked her up, hugging her tightly to his chest. Back in their room, he lay her sleeping body between them watching her breathe, inhaling her bubble bath smell.

"You know after the ordeal with finding my girl pregnant with someone else's kid, everything changed for me. All those deployments, all those missions I never once thought about having a family. I just assumed it was selfish of me to think that I could expect a woman to share this life. When I retired, I just didn't seem to want anyone permanently in my life. We were all sort of getting our new wheels beneath us, so to speak."

"What made you change your mind?" she asked linking their hands on the pillow above Calla's head.

"You. You and Ghost...I mean, I watched when Grace was brought here. Jesus she was so messed up and Ghost...that hard as nails, tough as shit man...he held her so lovingly, waited on her hand and foot. When they found out she was pregnant...it was like this switch went off inside me."

"Then I saw Doc and Bree fall for each other; then it was Whiskey and Kat; and when Angel eyes and Zulu connected...I don't know...I guess I just thought there must be someone out there for me. I knew I wasn't going to find it in a bar or anything. Then you walked into the gym." She smiled at him, kissing him sweetly over their daughters' body.

"God Darby, when I saw you...I just knew. It was like someone took a bat to my head. My mom always said that when I found her...I would feel as though the wind had been knocked from my body. She was right. Then I saw her," he said looking down at Calla. "I saw this sweet-faced, innocent, tinier version of you and all I could think about was wrapping you both in my arms and never letting go."

"Then do that Gunner," she said smiling at him. "Just wrap us in your arms and don't let go. Make me Mrs. Gunner Michaels next weekend and this little one Miss Calla Irene Michaels."

"Irene?" he whispered.

"Yea...I just thought it was pretty, so that's her middle name."

"Honey, that's my mothers' name. She goes by her middle name, Anne...but it's Irene Anne."

"Wow, that's strange," she grinned.

"This is going to be one spoiled little girl," he said smiling. "Get some sleep baby. I'm on watch." Darby was already closing her eyes when he pressed a soft kiss to the cheek of each of his girls. He was on watch. Permanently.

CHAPTER THIRTY-NINE

Gunner woke to find two little legs stretched across his stomach, the other half of the body resting against her mothers' stomach. He smiled, thanking God that he was able to wake up to this. Lifting Calla's body, he tried to move her without waking her, but her eyes popped open wide staring straight into his own.

"I was waiting for you," she whispered.

"You were?" he said kissing her on the forehead. He lifted her and placed a finger against his lips. "Let's let mommy sleep. Why were you waiting for me?"

"I want to make pancakes for breakfast before I go to school," she said as he took her downstairs. Gunner's stomach bottomed out at the thought of her going to school today. He remembered what Darby said last night and knew he had to let her feel normal, but it was killing him.

"Okay sweet girl, we'll make pancakes and then I'll take you to school, okay?" She nodded, her long brown hair flopping into her face. She pushed it back and he smiled, helping her push the hair from her face.

"Daddy?" she asked quietly.

"Yea baby."

"Will there be more bad men out there?" Gunner stopped in his tracks and looked back at his daughter. Lifting her from the counter, he walked with her to the sofa sitting with her in his arms.

"Calla honey, I'm going to be really honest and talk to you like a grown up, okay? There will always be bad men out there. But you know what?" Her little head shook vigorously, hair flying everywhere. "Good men will always stop them. Men like uncle Tango and Razor."

"And you daddy?" she asked.

"And me baby. Know this my sweet girl...daddy will always be here to protect you...always." He knew there might come a day when he couldn't do that, but by God he would die trying.

"Okay daddy...I just wanted to check. Will you make me pancakes now? I'm gonna go get dressed." He laughed as she took off toward her room racing passed Darby.

"Morning mommy!" she yelled.

"Morning Calla...no running." She looked at Gunner and grinned. "Let me guess, she bribed you to make pancakes."

"There was no bribery...I offered," he said smiling, laying a big kiss on her lips. "Come on babe...let's eat and meet the others."

An hour later they walked into the kitchen where everyone waited for hugs from Calla. She jumped at Razor first, hugging him fiercely and kissing his cheek, then jumped to George, reminding him of their Betsy Ross cupcakes. Making her way around the room, she stopped and looked once more.

"Where is uncle Tango?" she asked with a quivering lip.

"He's fine honey, he's at the hospital with Miss Taylor. She's not feeling well," said Darby.

"Oh...okay. Will he still be able to come to my play?" she asked.

"Of course, I will," said the booming voice from behind her. Calla jumped into Tango's arms kissing his cheeks, making raspberry noises and laughing. He smiled, but there was a sadness in his eyes that was like a gut punch to his brothers.

"Calla? Honey, why don't you let mommy and uncle Hawk take you to school today?" said Darby looking at Gunner who nodded.

"Okay mommy...bye daddy...by uncles." She giggled all the way down the long hallway. As Darby passed Tango she stood on her tiptoes and kissed his cheek.

"Thank you Tango." He nodded, smiling at the little woman.

"Coffee?" asked George holding out the mug. He took the cup and sat at the end of the table, his whiskers rough, his eyes creased with lines, lack of sleep visible in his features.

"How is she brother?" asked Gunner. Tango shrugged, biting his lower lip.

"She's...she's fucked up...she's hurtin' bad. Fucker really did a number on her. He was only alone with her for like five minutes and nearly killed her. Plastic surgeon fixed her nose and eye socket. The rest will heal in time."

"That's good, right?" asked Zulu.

"Yea. What we didn't know...none of us knew until Bree talked to her this morning...she'd been taken once before as a teenager."

"Fuuucck!" growled Ghost.

"Yea...that's almost exactly what I said," he tried to grin but just couldn't manage it. "She was taken by her step-brother...raped and beaten for days before the police found her. It's why she was here with her grandparents so much; she couldn't stand to be at home."

"Jesus brother, what can we do?" asked Gunner.

"Not sure yet. She said she wanted some time to think...time alone, so..." He shrugged, his big hands in the air and then slamming back to the table.

"Give her time Tango," said Grace. "I'll see if she'll let me visit today. Maybe we could get her to come back here when she gets released...make her feel safe again."

"Yea...that would be great Gracie. Thank you." They heard the big steel door slam and turned to see Skull.

"What did I miss?" he asked. The room laughed nervously, waving him to a seat.

"We'll tell you later," said Gunner. "What happened with Olivia and the charity function?"

"Boring as shit is what it was. Rented a fucking monkey suit and everything. Bunch of pretentious pricks...bitches with more money than common sense." He winced looking at Grace and Kat. "Sorry Gracie...not you and Kat."

"I understand," said Kat. "I've had to attend a few of those, and your description is pretty accurate."

"Anyway, I watched to see if she was approached by anyone, made any calls and nothing. I made the decision to approach her on my own. Told her I was a friend of Darby's and wanted to be sure she wasn't going to interfere in her life. Woman looked as though I'd flashed nude photos of her to the room. She pulled me aside and said she'd already forgotten about Darby and her escapade of deceit."

"Escapade of deceit? The fuck?" said Gunner.

"Said she figured with Darby running away from everything she was offering her and the girl, that she must have been right to assume the little girl was not her sons. Bitch actually told all her friends of the 'treachery' that she suffered at Darby's hands."

"You have got to be fucking kidding me?" said Gunner. "I'm not sure whether to be happy about this or to kill the bitch."

"I'd be happy brother. She has no intentions of coming near Darby or Calla. As far as she's concerned, they were never a part of her life. I went to the mansion…big as fuck all…said I was doing some contractor work for the old woman. Looked in every damn room…not one had toys, dolls, nothing. There is no sign of a child ever living there. She wiped them out brother and if I were you, I'd be fucking thrilled as shit for that."

"Damn…I just can't believe she would do that, but I guess gift horse and all that shit," said Gunner.

"Yea man," said Zulu holding Wade in his arms. "Now you can focus on getting married and raising that little girl as yours…the way God intended if you ask me." Gunner nodded smiling.

"Room for one more at this table?" asked Admiral Crossing.

"Geez…who let the riff-raff in?" said Zulu.

"Who would believe someone would marry your ass and actually give you children?" he remarked staring at the big man. Gabi looked up at the man and his eyes grew wide. "Wow…you hit the lottery didn't you Zulu?"

"Yes sir…I believe we all did."

"Hello, I'm Grace…married to Ghost," she said with an extended hand.

"Kat...married to Whiskey," said the other woman.

"What the hell? Maybe I need to hang out here for a while," he said smiling at the women. "Boys, I was hoping you'd have a few minutes for me this morning." Ghost nodded pointing the way to the conference room. As they all took their seats, Admiral Crossing cleared his throat.

"You boys did a nice job of stopping this shit show from getting worse. Wouldn't have expected anything less."

"Thanks Mike," said Ghost grinning at the man. "But I know you didn't come all the way out here from your fine home in D.C. to tell us we did a good job."

"You always were a smart-ass," he smiled. "No...you're right. President got wind of what you boys stopped. He was impressed that you did it without help from any of the alphabet agencies. I explained to him what you used to do, and he was intrigued."

"Hold it right there," said Gunner. "We're retired. Forced to retire actually. I'm not active duty and I won't be again."

"Nope...not asking for that."

"Then what are you asking for?" said Whiskey.

"I'm asking you to consider...on occasion...unofficially helping the country with things similar to this issue. I would be your liaison with the President and the President only. He would fund everything, and you would get contractor wages." Ghost never moved, never looked at his teammates once. He knew they were doing the same thing, staring down the older man.

"Why would we do this?" asked Gunner.

"Because we still need men like you," he said with honesty in his voice. "We won't send you to any foreign countries, we won't ask you to fight terrorists in their backyard, but we may ask you to fight them in ours. Gather intel, find ways inside using the club as your cover...something along those lines."

"What do we get for this besides a little extra coin?" asked Zulu. "Which by the way...as you can see...we don't really need."

"State of the art everything. Weapons, security, phones...you name the toy and I'll give it to you. Even let Ace improve upon it. Nothing will be traced to you and nothing will be traced to the government. You boys seem to have an affinity for helping the underdog. Well, this gives you the chance to do that and get paid well for it. You get to say yes or no to the missions...no questions asked...no backlash. It will all be in your control."

Ghost let out a long sigh and looked at his teammates.

"We're a team...we decide as a team," he said as they nodded. "Give us until after the holiday."

"Done. You have my contact and just so you boys know...I'd be damned proud to work with you again." Admiral Crossing left the room and they all looked from one face to the other. Whiskey finally stood and stared at his teammates.

"So, what time do the unicorns and leprechauns show up?"

CHAPTER FORTY

"Mom? Let the poor woman go, will you?" said Gunner as his mother held Darby so tightly, he could see her face turning red.

"Oh, leave me alone," she said pulling back to look at her. Anne Michaels was a very attractive older woman, her dark hair streaked with silver making her look regal. Her brown eyes were the same as her sons, all three of them. Ranger Michaels was the spitting image of his sons other than the snow-white hair. He was tall and well-built for his years, with wide shoulders and a straight, strong back.

"Darby you're simply stunning honey...absolutely stunning," she said kissing her cheek again. Ranger pushed his wife out of the way and grabbed Darby, hugging her and kissing her cheek.

"Thank you, Mrs. Michaels," she said breathlessly.

"Just Anne honey and where is my granddaughter?" she asked looking around the big green space behind the club.

"Here she comes," said Darby. "Calla? Calla honey come here." Calla ran towards her mother and stopped, her long brown hair with big curls and a huge white bow at the back. She had on one of her favorites dresses and was smiling big at Gunner.

"Calla...this is..."

"We're your grandparents honey," said Ranger kneeling down.

"You are!?" she asked with a gasp. Ranger laughed pulling her into a big bear hug.

"We are," he said laughing. "You can just call me grandpa or grandpa Ranger, and this is..."

"Move out of my way," said Anne pushing her husband aside. "Hello sweet child. I'm your grandma and I brought so many presents for you!"

"You did?" said Calla's eyes growing huge.

"Calla, what do you say?" said Darby.

"Thank you, grandma and grandpa!" She hugged them tightly and then looked at the two men standing beside them. "Are you, my uncles?"

"We are," laughed Striker. "And this is your aunt Laura."

"Wow...I have two more uncles and an aunt," she whispered.

"Yes, but I'm the coolest uncle," said Striker pulling a bag from his shoulder. He reached inside and pulled out a replica of one of his boats.

"This will float in the water and you can drive it from this little machine. I'll show you how."

"Whoa! Daddy look!" she yelled.

"I see baby," said Gunner looking up to see his mothers' eyes fill with tears.

"Well, I think I'm the coolest uncle," said Hunter. From inside his bag, he pulled out a huge puppy, his head all black and brown, his big paws already making Gunner think twice about the gift.

"A puppy! A puppy! Mommy, uncle Hunter got me a puppy!" she yelled.

"Yes, I can see that," she said crossing her arms. "I wonder if uncle Hunter is going to be around to train and feed the puppy and pick up the piles he leaves." Hunter laughed, holding up his hands.

"I'm only here to be the favorite uncle...not the favorite brother or brother-in-law," he said laughing.

"Well, when is this wedding?" asked Anne.

"We're actually doing it this afternoon at the courthouse so we can get Calla's name changed at the same time," said Gunner. Anne smiled down at Calla and a tear slipped from her cheek again. Darby wasn't sure if they were happy tears or sad tears.

"Anne...you're making the poor girl nervous," said Ranger.

"Oh...oh sweetheart...these are happy tears. I can already tell how much Gunner loves you both and that you love him. I'm so happy for the two of you. Does she have...is her..." Darby shook her head.

"My ex-husband wasn't really part of her life, but he died about a year ago. His mother wants nothing to do with us, so I'm afraid you are crowned favorite grandparents without even trying."

"I can live with that," said Ranger. "Calla? What are we going to name the puppy?"

"Yea, Calla," said Hunter, "what will you name him? He's yours, so you have to feed him, and walk him, and train him." Hunter set the puppy down and handed her the leash. She was already struggling to hold the ball of muscle.

"Hmmm...let me see. Daddy is Gunner, grandpa is Ranger...that's a cool kind of soldier, uncle Hawk told me."

"He did, did he?" said Darby looking at Hawk across the lawn. "Mommy might have to talk to uncle Hawk about appropriate discussions with a four-year-old."

"Okay…and then I have uncle Hunter…and uncle Striker…so I think he should be named Bullitt."

"Bullitt?" said Darby. "Gunner? Seriously?"

"What? I didn't tell her to name him that! She's a very intuitive little girl."

"Bullitt come here," called Calla. Darby watched as the damned dog ran right to her, jumping into her arms and licking her face. Frustrated, she blew out a breath and waved her arms.

"Fine…Bullitt it is. Just what kind of dog is that and how big will he be?" she asked Hunter.

"Well…I got him from a friend who runs sled dogs in Alaska. He was part of a litter of pups. The mom was a German shepherd and the dad as Burmese mountain dog."

"Wait…aren't those dogs like huge?" asked Darby.

"Ummm...yea babe," said Gunner. "You can tell by his paws and his ears he's going to be a big one but think of it like an extra layer of protection for Calla."

"Hunter...you might just be my least favorite uncle right now," said Darby with her arms crossed.

"Naw, you'll learn to love me," he said kissing his sister-in-law's cheek. "Besides, he'll probably only grow to be one-twenty or one-thirty." Darby gasped, but before she could say anything Gunner spoke.

"Alright everyone, I need to marry my girl and then we're going to celebrate!" said Gunner waving at everyone to follow them to the vehicles. Two hours later Mr. and Mrs. Gunner Michaels and their daughter, Calla Irene Michaels were eating cake and opening presents. For every wedding gift the couple received, Calla received a gift.

Ranger was off to the side speaking with George, the man closest to his age, while Anne doted on her new granddaughter, already planning trips to the amusement parks near their home in Florida. Toward the end of the evening, an exhausted and drained looking Tango finally showed.

"Hey man, how is she?" asked Gunner.

"Same. We got her settled upstairs near my room, but she doesn't really want to see me." Tango shrugged his shoulders as if it didn't bother him, but Gunner knew that it damned sure did.

"She'll get there brother, give her time." He nodded and then turned back to the barn to head to his room. He stopped outside Taylor's room and knocked softly.

"Come in," came the meek voice.

"I was just making sure everything was okay...do you need anything?" he asked keeping his distance. Her face was swollen and black and blue, the features vastly different from what he remembered on the woman.

"No...no it's okay Tango. Tango...Tyler...why are you doing this? This wasn't your fault; you don't owe me anything."

"Not about owing shit, honey. It's about not protecting you when I should have. This is my fault and I should have been there." She shook her head from side to side slowly, careful not move too quickly.

"Not your fault," she said.

"It is and every time I look at you, I see the mistakes I made." Taylor felt the tears in her eyes and turned away.

"I'm tired. I think I want to be alone now," she said. He nodded, closing the door and went across the hall to his own room. She deserved whatever she wanted as far as he was concerned. If she wanted peace and quiet, he would give it to her. If she wanted a new house, he'd buy it for her. He was already working on getting the shop back up and running.

He would give her anything she wanted.

CHAPTER FORTY-ONE

The noise was nearly deafening at the breakfast table the next morning. George had to delicately tell Calla she could not bring Bullitt into the kitchen, which made her demand breakfast on the porch through tears that nearly killed poor old George. Her uncle Hunter was relegated to the space beside her for giving her the suggestion that Bullitt should enjoy breakfast with her.

Gunner and Darby were going to spend a few nights at the property on the Chesapeake and leave Calla in the capable hands of his parents and brothers. Tango walked downstairs looking around to see if Taylor decided to come down for breakfast, disappointment showing on his face when he didn't see her.

"I'll go check on her Tango," said Gabi smiling at him. He nodded his thanks as the woman disappeared upstairs. Gunner's sister-in-law was holding one of the twins, marveling at how big they were, feeling sorry for poor Gabi. Zulu could only nod and shrug, it wasn't his fault he was so damned big. Besides, Gabi wasn't exactly petite, it was her fault too.

"Tango," said Gabi standing in the doorway, "she's gone. Sh-she left you a note." Tango swallowed hard, looking around the room at the shocked faces.

"Read it," he said quietly. "Please." Gabi nodded.

Tyler – you were right—looking at me must be very difficult for you. You don't owe me anything. You saved me and saved Calla, you should be so proud of yourself. I'm going away for a while...I need to go away for a while. I'll be selling the business, so I might not ever be back. My only regret is I wish we had our date Tyler...I was really looking forward to finally kissing you...the only man I ever willingly wanted to kiss...desired to kiss. You deserve to be happy...find someone you can look at and feel happiness. Yours – Tay

"Fuck," he whispered. "She thought I couldn't look at her because of her injuries. I have to find her...I have to..." Ace poked his head in the door and smiled.

"Found her."

EXCERPT From TANGO

Tango couldn't believe she'd walked out on them. She was in pain and couldn't drive, so she had to have called for a ride. He drove in the direction that Ace told him she was located, eyeing the small little houses with their perfectly manicured lawns and flower beds. At the end of the cul-de-sac, he saw the yellow cab idling in the driveway. Stepping out of his truck he ran toward the car.

"You waiting for a blonde girl with bad bruises on her face?" he asked. The man looked him up and down, sneering.

"You hurt that little girl?" he asked.

"NO! Fuck no...I'm in love with her!" The man looked as though he didn't believe him, sneering again. "Listen, she's the love my life. I didn't hurt her. I need to protect her. Here, a hundred bucks for you to go." The man took the money and nodded.

Tango watched the cab pull away and wiped his hands on the front of his jeans. Walking toward the door, he knocked softly. A few minutes later, the door cracked open.

"I'm almost done..." she gasped. "Tango...what...why..."

"Because I'm in love with you Taylor. You misunderstood me. I didn't mean I couldn't look at your face because of the damage, I meant I couldn't look at it and not see all the things I did wrong. It's because of me you look like that honey. It's because of me you're in pain." Taylor felt the tears come and couldn't stop them. Tango pulled her into his body, holding her gently so as not to hurt her.

"Oh Tango...how can you love me? You know...you know what my stepbrother did. I'm broken...I'm so broken," she sobbed.

"We're all broken honey, some of us are broken in big pieces, easy to put back together. Others have a million little pieces that take time to be put back together. Doesn't matter to me which you are. I want to be there for you Taylor...help you. Please don't turn me away...please."

"You said you love me...how..." Tango laughed and kissed her lips gently.

"I have no idea how my love, all I know is it happened and I'm not letting you go Taylor. I can't baby...I just would die." He held her while she cried in his arms, rubbing soft, lazy circles on her back. "Come back with me...you don't have to stay in the barn...stay in my house. Please."

"Okay," she nodded. "Okay Tango."

Other Books by Mary Kennedy you might enjoy!

REAPER Security Series

Erin's' Hero
Lauren's Warrior
Lena's' Mountain
Sara's' Chance
Mary's Angel
Kari's Gargoyle
Rachelle's Savior
Adele's Heart
Tori's' Secret
Montana Rules
Savannah Rain
Gray Skies
My First Choice
Three Wishes
Second Chances
One Day at a Time
When You Least Expect It
Missing Hearts

Trail of Love

The Gifted Series

Dark Visions
Dark Medicine
Dark Flame

My SEAL Boys (connections to the REAPER Series)

Ian
Noa
Carter
Lars
Trevor
Fitz
Chris
O'Hara

Steel Patriots MC

Ghost – Book One
Doc – Book Two
Whiskey – Book Three
Zulu – Book Four

ABOUT THE AUTHOR

Mary Kennedy is the mother of two adult children and grandmother to two beautiful grandsons. She works full-time at a job she loves and writing is her creative outlet. She lives in Texas and enjoys traveling, reading, and cooking. Her passion for assisting veterans and veteran causes comes from a strong military family.

Dear Readers,

I love hearing from you and encourage you to visit my website insatiableink.squarespace.com. Leave me your thoughts and ideas on new books or expanding on characters. It's also a safe space to give your own feelings, similar to those of the characters. I look forward to hearing from you and hope you enjoy other books in my collections.

Explore...and enjoy!

Made in the USA
Monee, IL
19 September 2021